Also published in Large Print
by Erle Stanley Gardner:

The Adventures of Paul Pry

VOLUME 2

Erle Stanley Gardner

G.K.HALL & CO.
Boston, Massachusetts
1991

Published in Large Print by arrangement with
The Mysterious Press/Warner Books, Inc.

G.K. Hall Large Print Book Series.

Set in 16 pt. Plantin.

Library of Congress Cataloging-in-Publication Data
(Revised for vol. 2)

Gardner, Erle Stanley, 1889–1970.
    The adventures of Paul Pry.

    (A Nightingale mystery in large print) (G.K. Hall
large print book series)
    "A large print mystery"—Cover.
    1. Pry, Paul (Fictitious character)—Fiction.
2. Detective and mystery stories, American. 3. Large
type books. I. Title. II. Series
PS3513.A6322A66 1991   813'.52   90-5097
ISBN 0-8161-5105-9 (lg. print : v. 1)
ISBN 0-8161-5106-7 (lg. print : v. 2)

Contents

Slick and Clean

Death awaited him in that mysterious chamber—death from three blunt-nosed guns. Yet Paul Pry only smiled as he hurried toward it. When a fellow has been put on the spot, the least he can do is to be on time for the works.

—1—

Screams in the Dark

The girl emerged from the underbrush by the river road, stood where the headlights of the automobile fell full upon her white face, and screamed with stark terror.

Such clothes as she had worn had been ripped to shreds. There were bruises on her arms and chest. The white skin of her body was scratched where brush had scraped against it as she had plunged headlong in mad terror.

Her eyes were staring, dark with fear. Her face was pale to the lips. One well-formed leg protruded through a rip which ran from the hem of her skirt to the hip. Her hands were upraised, palms outward, and ostentatiously empty.

But Paul Pry did not bring his automobile to an immediate stop. Big Front Gilvray, arch-gangster, had decreed that Paul Pry be placed on the spot, and the decree had been overlong in execution.

The sixteen cylinder automobile which

Paul Pry was driving was no mere sedan, as its appearance would indicate. It was built of armor which would stop a rifle bullet, and the windows were of bullet-proof glass.

Several slight indentations in the armor of the body bore witness to a previous attempt on the part of the gangsters to carry out the orders of their vengeful chief. But the machine gun had failed to penetrate and Paul Pry had lived to take his powerful car out for an evening drive on the river road.

And because it was more than probable that this screaming woman might well be the bait with which some trap was to be sprung, Paul Pry ran his automobile some fifty yards past her before he brought it to a stop. Then he switched off all lights, took the butt of his automatic in his hand, and opened the door.

"Do you want help?" he called.

And, as his hail was swallowed up in the dark shadows of the brush which rimmed the road, Paul Pry listened, his every sense alert.

The screams of the woman came to his ears. They were steady, high-pitched, mechanical screams. Such screams might a woman give who had gone into hysterics, then worn down her emotions through a sheer ecstasy of fear until fatigue had taken a hand and made of the screams a regular rhythm of unconscious effort.

Paul Pry called to her again, and the call was unanswered. But the screams became louder. She was running toward him.

Paul pry left the door open. He started the purring power of the sixteen cylinder motor, waited.

She was still screaming as she blocked the door of the automobile.

"Get in," said Paul Pry.

The woman scrambled in the car. Paul Pry snapped in the clutch so suddenly that the forward lunge of the machine slammed the door shut. His headlights snapped on, and he also clicked on the dome light—just to make sure that those hands remained empty.

They were still empty, beseeching hands that clung to his coat with the grip of hysteria. The screams ceased, and, in their place, came sobs, heart-wrenching sobs which would eventually bring solace to the overtaxed nerves.

Paul Pry drove his machine for nearly a mile, then turned up a side road and stopped. He disengaged his left hand from the steering wheel, turned toward her.

She grabbed him, flung her slender body close to his as a drowning woman will grasp at the form of a rescuer. Paul Pry slid his right arm around her waist. She pressed a tear-stained cheek to his, sobbed out unintelligible words.

Paul Pry patted the bare shoulder, attempted to soothe her. Gradually his words impressed themselves upon her senses and the throbbing quieted. She snuggled to him as a kitten might snuggle to a warm brick, dropped her head upon his shoulder, and lapsed into a semi-conscious condition which seemed half sleep, half stupor.

Paul Pry, engine idling for a quick getaway if occasion should require, lights switched off, right hand within quick reaching distance of his automatic, maintained watchful silence.

After some ten minutes she straightened. Her muscles seemed more relaxed. Her hands ceased to claw at his garments.

"Who are you?" she asked.

"The name," he said, "Pry. You seemed to be pretty much frightened."

She flung herself to him as he reminded her of her fright. Then, as his hand slid along the bare skin of her back where the garments had been torn, she gasped and flung herself away, modesty asserting itself.

She explored the damage to her garments with questing fingers.

"Isn't there a light in the car?" she asked.

"Yes," answered Paul Pry, "there is a dome light."

"Turn it on."

He snapped the switch.

As the light showed her the extent of her figure which was readily visible through the torn garments, she stifled a little scream.

"Turn it off!" she cried.

Paul Pry switched off the light.

"Haven't you a robe or something?"

"I have an overcoat in the back of the car. I'll get it."

"Don't bother," she said, and was over the back of the seat with a motion as lithe as that of a wildcat stalking from cover to cover.

Paul Pry turned on the light again.

"On the robe rail," he said.

"O.K., big boy, keep your head turned."

There was a rustle of garments.

"That's better," she said. "Lord, what a spectacle I must have been! Did you find me in the road?"

"You came to the road and stopped me."

"Where are we now?"

"About a mile from where I picked you up."

"Let's get out of here—quick!"

"Do you want to tell me about it? That is, can I help?" asked Paul Pry.

She climbed back over the seat, gathered the overcoat about her legs, wrapped it around her breast, grinned.

"O.K. Gimme a cigarette. Guess I must have gone off my nut for a while."

"You had hysterics."

"Maybe. I ain't the type that can't stand the gaff, but that was too much. They were taking me for a ride."

Paul Pry handed her the electric cigarette lighter. She inhaled a great drag from the cigarette, blew out the smoke in twin streams from appreciative nostrils, sighed.

"Let's go," she said.

Paul Pry nosed the car over the rough road, found a good place to turn, swung the big machine around, headed back to the highway, and purred into speed.

"Shoot," he said.

She cocked her head on one side, regarded him with quizzical eyes. They were, he saw, blue eyes, eyes that held a sort of light in their depths, a puzzling, challenging light. Her lips were half parted, and pearly teeth glinted invitingly. Her head was tilted back and up, and the long line of her throat, stretching down to where his overcoat lapels parted, showed with the gleam of pure ivory.

"I'm not a *good* girl," she said, and watched him.

Paul Pry laughed.

"What is this, a confession?"

She took another drag at the cigarette, shook her head, removed the paper cylinder and smiled frankly.

"No, but I don't want to get you in bad, and I wanted to tell you the worst at the start. I'm a gangster's moll—or I was. I've helped rum-runners load and unload, and I've seen a hijacking or two."

Paul Pry did not seem greatly surprised.

"So," she stressed, "I'm not what you'd call a 'good' girl."

Paul Pry's eyes were on the road ahead.

"The habit of classifying all women as either 'good' or 'bad' went out of fashion ten or fifteen years ago—thank heavens!" he said.

She sighed.

"I'm glad you feel that way. You see, I

9

was the moll of Harry the Dip, and they took me for a ride. Maybe you read about it in yesterday's paper. Well, they thought I might get sore and squeal, so they decided to take me for a ride.

"I was to visit a girl friend and stay with her for a while. She said she'd send a friend in his car. God, she double-crossed me! Damn her. I'll claw her eyes out. Well, that's about all there was to it. This 'friend' jabbed a gun in my ribs. The car stopped and picked up another man. They took me out on the river road, turned up a side road, found a place that suited them, and got ready to bump me off.

"But I got a break. One of them sort of fell for me. I got to playing them one against the other, watched my chance and jumped into the brush. They both shot at me half a dozen times, and I guess the fear and the running and all that just sent me off my nut. I don't remember anything else until I found myself pulling the cry-baby act on your shoulder. Was I a nuisance?"

"Not at all," said Paul Pry.

She sighed.

"God, it's awful lonesome with Harry gone!"

Paul Pry made no comment. The blue

10

eyes flashed up and down his profile. The overcoat fell away on one side, disclosing a large expanse of shapely limb. But the eyes of Paul Pry, narrowed into calculating slits, remained on the road.

Slowly, with a tardiness that was almost an invitation, the girl replaced the flap of the overcoat and regarded him thoughtfully.

"Are you afraid of getting mixed up with the gangs just for rescuing me?"

Paul Pry answered that at once.

"No," he said.

"I didn't think you would be."

"What's your name?" he asked her.

"Louise Eckhart," she told him. Then, after a moment, "My friends call me Lou."

"Where do you want to go, Lou?"

She smiled up at him.

"I like you," she said.

He nodded. "Where to?" he repeated.

"I've got a suitcase parked at the Union Depot. I did have the check in my stocking. Wonder if it's gone?"

She pulled the overcoat to one side, searched the tops of her stockings, first the right, then the left. She handed him a crumpled bit of pasteboard.

"That's luck. I can get some clothes. Would you mind driving to the depot, get-

11

ting the suitcase, and then driving me where I can dress?"

"Not at all," said Paul Pry. "I'd better get some gasoline if we're going that far, though. I'm about out."

They were approaching the junction of the river road with the through boulevard, and the lights of gasoline stations flung themselves out across the darkness.

The girl sighed.

"You," she proclaimed, "are a regular guy."

Paul Pry made no comment. He drove into a gasoline station.

"Fill her up," he told the attendant, and walked to the telephone, gave the number of his apartment, and heard the voice of "Mugs" Magoo on the telephone.

"Drunk, Mugs?"

"Not yet. Gimme ten minutes more an' I will be."

"Forget it. Take a drink of water and chase down to the Union Depot. I'm going to drive in there with a moll. Manage to give her the once-over and see if you place her. Then go back to the apartment. I'll meet you there."

Mugs Magoo grunted.

"I'll do it all for you—all except take the

drink of water," he remarked. "Water's poison to my system," and he clicked the receiver back in place.

―2――――――――――――――――――――

The Goose Cackles

Paul Pry paid the attendant. The girl watched him with shrewd eyes. "Telling the wife you were detained at the office?" she asked.

"No wife."

"Betcha I'm making you miss a heavy date, then."

Paul Pry grinned.

"It's worth it."

He got into the car, drove rapidly and skillfully through the traffic, parked in front of the Union Depot, handed a red-cap porter the crumpled pasteboard and a half dollar.

"At the check stand," he said. "Make it snappy."

And Paul Pry watched the face of the girl at his side to see if she was at all nonplused at his failure to call for the suitcase in person. If she was, she failed to show it.

Paul Pry was red hot. It might well be that the sole function of this girl was to get him on the spot in front of the checking stand at the Union Depot.

Mugs Magoo walked past.

His glassy eyes flicked once toward the automobile, then turned away. He walked awkwardly, dressed in shabby clothes, his right arm gone at the shoulder.

At one time he had known every crook in the underworld, and his information was now hardly less complete. He had been "camera-eye" man for the metropolitan police. A political shake-up, an accident which cost him his right arm, and bad booze, had made him a human derelict selling pencils in the gutter.

Paul Pry had "discovered" him, and organized a strange partnership. For Mugs Magoo never forgot a name, a face or a connection. While Paul Pry was an opportunist de luxe who lived by his wits. And of late he had chosen to exercise those wits in a battle against Benjamin Franklin Gilvray, known to the police as Big Front Gilvray.

For years Big Front Gilvray had grown in power and prestige. The police knew him as a big man, too powerful to tackle, a gangster who was always in the background, letting his minions do the dirty work of murder and plunder. The police hated Gilvray, and they feared him.

To Paul Pry, Big Front Gilvray was merely the goose which laid his golden eggs.

The red cap returned with a suitcase, deposited it in the car. Paul Pry drove away into the stream of traffic.

"Gosh," said the girl, "I can't change in here. You're sort of one of the family, but these windows are too wide. I don't want to give the whole damned city a treat."

Paul Pry nodded.

"We will go to a safe place," he said.

And he meant what he said. He had no intention of letting this girl open that suitcase, take out a gun and pull the trigger.

He took her to a cheap hotel, engaged a suite of connecting rooms, took her up to those rooms, and closed the door while she engaged in the process of changing her clothes.

When she rejoined him in the bedroom, Paul Pry was ready for anything in the line of attack. But there was nothing. She smiled gratefully at him.

"Kid," she said, giving him her hand, "here's where we part. I ain't asked you nothing about yourself, but I have an idea you're a big shot on the lam, maybe from Chi. It's easy enough to see that you're about half sold on the idea that I am a lure to put you on the spot.

"But you've been a gent, and you've treated me white. I'm going out. I won't see you again. Tonight at eleven o'clock I've got to go up against the most dangerous thing I've ever tackled. If you read in the papers about me being found with a lot of lead in me, remember that I was thinkin' of you when I cashed in.

"You've given me a chance, and you've been on the up and up. Want to drive me downtown?"

He nodded. "You'll stay here tonight?"

"If I come through alive."

"Must you run into it?"

"Yes. I'm meeting a big shot of the Gilvray gang in the Mandarin Cafe. He's got Room 13 reserved. If I can get what I want I'll walk in and walk out inside of five minutes. If I ain't out by then I'll never come out. But I've got to go. That big shot has something I've got to have."

Paul Pry lit a cigarette.

"Just you and he alone?" he asked.

"That's the bargain. I wouldn't deal any other way. It's a long chance, but I'm taking it. Big Front Gilvray doesn't waste any love on me. My man was a thorn in his flesh. He'd like to give me the works. But he needs me in his business. He's pulling a job that they've got to have a moll on that knows the ropes. I'm elected. I can deliver the goods. The other molls can't.

"I wish to God Harry hadn't been bumped. Then I wouldn't worry. If I had a man to cover me, I'd walk in there. If I wasn't out in five minutes my man could brush in through the curtains with his rod ready, and take me out.

"The Gilvray gangster's yellow. He's Chick Bender. Used to be a mouthpiece until he got disbarred. Now he's the brains of the gang, but he's got no guts."

Paul Pry nodded.

"Yes, I've heard of Chick Bender."

The girl yawned and pulled her cupped hands along the contour of her leg, frankly straightening the seam in her stocking without bothering to turn her back.

"Yeah," she remarked. "You ain't heard anything good about him."

Paul Pry switched off the lights. "You have the keys," he said.

She kissed him in the dark.

"Baby, you're a regular guy. Wish I knew

you better. Maybe you'd help me give the Gilvray gang a double-crossing that would make a fortune for us. God, I wish Harry hadn't got on the spot."

Paul Pry patted her shoulder.

"What time's the appointment?"

"Eleven. Wish me luck."

"You've got it. It's early yet. Want to drive around?"

"No, just dump me—tell you what, big boy, if you want to see more of me, stick around the Mandarin about five after eleven. If I come through O.K. I'll give you a tumble. If I get bumped you can forget about me."

Her blue eyes were wistful.

"I'd sure like to see more of you," she added.

Paul Pry smiled at her.

"Perhaps, if you find yourself in danger, you may find me sticking around."

"You mean it?"

"Perhaps."

Her arms twined around his neck in a fierce embrace.

Mugs Magoo emptied the glass of whiskey with a single motion of the left arm. His glassy eyes fastened upon Paul Pry in emotionless appraisal.

"You got no business here," he said.

Paul Pry laughed, entered the apartment and closed the steel door.

"Why so? Isn't it my apartment?"

"Yeah. I guess so, but you ain't got no business being here. You'd oughta be out pushing daisies. You got a date with the undertaker. How'd you break it?"

Paul Pry took off his top coat and hat, came over and sat down.

"Meaning?" he said.

Mugs Magoo poured himself another drink of whiskey.

"Meaning that the moll was Maude Ambrose. She went by the nickname of Maude the Musher in Chi. That's because she's got such a good line of mush. She usually lets a guy rescue her from some danger or other. Then she gets mushy over him and finally puts him on the spot."

Paul Pry lit a cigarette. Twin devils were dancing in his eyes.

"She's nothing but a kid," he objected.

"Kid, hell! She's a kidder."

"You think she's tied up with Gilvray's gang?"

Mugs Magoo sighed, poured himself a

19

drink of whiskey, gazed at the bottle ruefully.

"Hell," he said, "it's a cinch. You never would follow my advice. First you twist Gilvray's tail into a knot, and then instead of crawlin' into a hole an' pullin' the hole in after you, you start raggin' hell outa Gilvray.

"Nobody's goin' to stand that. An' then, on top of it all, you drive around just like you was any ordinary citizen out for a little air. Gilvray's found out your car is bullet proof. He's fixed up somethin' else for you. Maude the Musher!

"I presume you found her in her undies, just climbin' from the river where she claimed somebody'd tried to drown her, didn't you? That's her best line, getting all roughed up and losin' most of her clothes, then fallin' on the neck of the guy she's ropin' and gettin' mushy."

Paul Pry puffed at the cigarette with every evidence of enjoyment.

"You have described almost exactly what happened, Mugs."

Mugs Magoo blinked his glassy expressionless eyes.

"Yeah. Her man's in town, too."

"Her man?"

"Yeah, Charles Simmons. They call him

Charley the Checker, because he always works a suitcase checking racket wherever he goes. He's bought into the checking concession at the Union Depot. That's where the Jane had her suitcase parked.

"When you handed the red cap the ticket for that suitcase it was her way of lettin' her man know that you'd fallen for her line. So they got the spot ready for you.

"I didn't ever expect to see you again. So I came back an' tried to get drunk. But I can't make the grade. Not yet, I can't. I ain't had but about an hour, though."

And Mugs Magoo poured the last of the whiskey in the quart bottle into the glass, tossed it off, looked significantly at the empty bottle, then at Paul Pry.

That individual laughed, took a key from his pocket, tossed it to Mugs.

"Here's the key to the whiskey safe. Go as far as you like, Mugs. I'm to be put on the spot tonight at eleven."

"Huh, she put it off that long, eh?"

"Yes. I'm to be punctured at Room 13 at the Mandarin Cafe at exactly eleven-five."

Mugs Magoo blinked his glassy eyes rapidly.

"Then you keep off the streets tonight. You stay right here."

21

Paul Pry consulted his thin watch.

"On the contrary, Mugs, I think I shall be on my way to keep my appointment with the undertaker."

He got to his feet.

"You mean you're goin' to fall for Maude the Musher an' walk on the spot?"

Paul Pry nodded.

"Yes. I rather think I have use for this girl you call Maude the Musher. She offers a point of contact with the Gilvray gang. And I have a hunch they're about ready to do something."

Mugs Magoo's jaw sagged.

"Do something—Hell, you don't mean—"

Paul Pry nodded as he wrapped a scarf about his neck.

"Exactly, Mugs. I have decided to let the goosie lay another golden egg."

And Paul Pry was gone, the door slamming shut with a clicking of spring locks and bolts.

"I," observed Mugs Magoo, "will be damned!"

He blinked incredulous eyes at the door through which Paul Pry had vanished, and then bestirred himself to go to the safe where the whiskey was kept.

"I better get plenty while the stuff is

here," he observed to himself, his tongue getting a little thick. "Dealin' with an administrator is goin' to be hell!"

—3—

Embrace of Death

Charles Simmons, known in Chicago as Charley the Checker, sat in Room 13 at the Mandarin Cafe with a heavy caliber revolver on his lap. His right hand rested within a few inches of the gun butt.

Back of him, well to the right, sat Chick Bender, the disbarred lawyer, brains of the Gilvray gang. He was a hatchet-faced man with cold eyes, and the habit of constantly blinking and sniffing. His long bony nose twitched and sniffed, sniffed and twitched. Occasionally he sucked his under lip between his teeth and chewed on it nervously. He was ill at ease.

The girl sat at the table, her chin resting on her cupped hands, her blue eyes twinkling with lazy humor.

"So he fell? You're sure he fell?" asked Chick Bender.

The girl laughed, a throaty laugh of voluptuous abandon.

"Hell, yes," she said.

Charley the Checker glanced at his watch.

"He's supposed to be bad medicine, awful fast with a gun."

The girl's voice drawled out an insult.

"Gettin' yellow?"

The gangster sneered at her.

"Don't get fresh or you'll get knocked for a loop. You're getting altogether too certain of what a hell of a swell moll you are lately."

"Yeah?" she asked.

"Yeah," he said, and swept his right arm in a backhanded sweep. The knuckles caught her full on the chin and swept her head back, leaving a red spot on her lip where the teeth had bit through the skin.

Chick Bender stirred uneasily, frowning.

The girl's eyes flashed, but she choked back the words that came to her lips.

"Remember," warned Chick Bender. "Have your gun all ready. Don't give him a chance to get organized. Shoot as soon as he comes through the door."

A clock boomed the hour of eleven.

Below the green curtain appeared the silken pajamas of a Chinese waiter. The foot showed the typical shoe of the Chinese.

"You leady eatum?" asked a singsong voice as the waiter pushed through the curtain, set pots of tea on the table, put down bowls filled with thin rice cakes, each cake containing a printed slip of paper upon which had been printed an optimistic forecast of the future.

Charley the Checker slowly moved his right hand back.

"Yeah, but wait about ten minutes before you bring the rest of the stuff. Maybe somebody else comes."

"All light," said the waiter, and shuffled from the room.

The clock clacked off seconds which became minutes. Chick Bender lit a cigarette with a hand which shook. Charley the Checker looked at his watch and grunted.

"What the hell. It's seven after eleven right now. I bet you fell down on the job, Maude."

The girl sucked the blood from her lip.

"I hope to God I did," she snapped.

Charley the Checker sneered. "It'll give you what you've been needin' for a long while when we get done with this guy," he said. "Now remember the getaway, you guys—"

He broke off as footsteps sounded along

the rough board floor. His hand crept down to his gun.

"I'm goin' to let him have it as soon as he steps in," he said. "Get ready. We ain't takin' any chances with this baby."

The footsteps drew nearer, seemed to hesitate for a moment, then the form loomed against the curtain. Charley the Checker raised his right hand, the gun concealed beneath a napkin. The girl leaned forward, lips parted, eyes gleaming. Chick Bender pressed himself back against his chair as though to make himself as inconspicuous as possible.

The curtains bulged inward as a form pressed against it, pushed it to one side. And Charley sighed, lowered his hand. Chick Bender took a deep breath. The girl's lips came together.

For the legs which were visible beneath the green of the curtain were encased in silken pajamas, and the shoes were those of the Chinese, flat, formless shoes topped with black velvet upon which were embroidered red and green dragons.

The curtain came to one side. A huge tray, piled high with smoking dishes, obscured the upper portion of the waiter.

It was the girl who first noticed that the

26

hand which held the tray was not yellow, but white. She gasped. Charley the Checker, his own eyes caught by some incongruity of costume, streaked his hand up from under the table.

At that precise moment Paul Pry lowered one end of the tray and the steaming dishes, the boiling soup, the hot tea, all cascaded down upon the gangster.

Red-hot chicken noodles caught him on a level with his throat. The soup drained down his collar, the noodles festooned themselves about his collar and down his vest, looping over the vest buttons.

A pot of hot tea fell squarely on his lap. Egg *foo yung ha* dropped onto his head and slipped back down his collar. He screamed with pain and leaned forward.

Paul Pry flipped his right hand over and down.

There was a rubber slungshot suspended from his wrist. It thunked upon the top of the gangster's head, and Charley the Checker became as utterly inert as a half-emptied sack of meal.

Chick Bender was on his feet, his eyes glassy, hands clawing nervously at his hip. Paul Pry scooped up a tea pot from the table and flung it with unerring aim.

The gangster tried to dodge, failed, and staggered back under the impetus of the blow. Hot tea dashed over him. He tore frantically at his garments as the hot liquid soaked through to the skin.

Paul Pry's right wrist arced through the air and Chick Bender stretched his length upon the floor. There were running steps. A yellow face surveyed the wreckage through the green curtain, uttered a wild volley of chattering words and disappeared.

Paul Pry grinned at the woman.

It took her a full breath to adjust herself to the suddenly changed situation. For an instant she seemed on the point of flashing her hand to her breast for some weapon. Paul Pry's voice steadied her.

"They double-crossed you, kid. I found out there were two of 'em in the room. You had told me your bargain called for meeting Chick Bender alone. Then when you didn't come out in five minutes like you said you would, I knew there was something wrong, and I came to rescue you."

The girl nodded. Slowly, a smile came over her features.

"My hero!" exclaimed Maude the Musher.

Paul Pry worked fast.

"You said one of them had something you wanted?"

Maude the Musher had not been entirely certain just what it was she had told Paul Pry, but she nodded affirmation. It was time when it was best to agree to anything.

Paul Pry dropped to his knees in front of Chick Bender. His hands parted the tea-soaked garments, went exploring in to the still hot pockets.

He pulled out a roll of bills, a wallet which contained papers, a note-book. Then he turned to Charley the Checker. Once more his hands darted through the pockets with uncanny skill and a swift precision which cut minutes to seconds, seconds to split fractions.

His collection of miscellaneous papers was augmented by another sheaf of currency, more letters and note-books.

"Let's go," said Paul Pry.

Maude the Musher had fully adjusted herself to the situation by this time. The trap had failed, but the bait was still good. It remained for her to string Paul Pry along until he could once more be lured on a hot spot.

"Dearest!" she said, and clutched him to her.

Paul Pry fought loose from the embrace.

"We've no time to lose," he said.

There was the sound of running feet in the corridor, the jabbering of many voices. A police whistle shrilled from the pavement. Paul Pry took the rolled currency which had come from Chick Bender, tossed it to one of the yellow men who led the procession.

"To pay for damage," he said.

The beady black eyes fastened upon the denomination of the outer bill in that roll, and suddenly widened with glittering glee. The man's swift fingers appraised the roll, called out sentences in the singsong Cantonese dialect, and a lane opened through which Paul Pry and the girl traveled.

There were heavy feet on the stairs.

"Police no likum," said Paul Pry.

The Chinaman who clutched the roll of bills nodded his head.

"Heavy savvy," he said. "You come."

He guided them through tortuous passages, up and down dark staircases until they finally reached the street at a point some two blocks from the Mandarin Cafe.

Paul Pry called a cab.

"Sweetheart!" said Maude the Musher,

and burrowed into his embrace. "I've never known a man like you, never, never, never!"

Paul Pry patted her shoulder.

The taxi rumbled through traffic, found its way to the hotel where Paul Pry had engaged the suite of rooms. He and the girl went up in the rickety elevator. Paul Pry unlocked the door, stood back for the girl to enter. She walked into his room, switched on the light, smiled at him.

"Dearest," she said, a catch in her voice, her eyes starry, "you've made me love you!"

Paul Pry shook his head.

"No. It's just gratitude. Your nerves have been all unstrung. You wait until tomorrow and see how you feel."

Her eyes blazed.

"You don't want my love, then!" she stormed, and flounced into her own room, slamming the door, bolting it.

Paul Pry grinned at the opportune display of temper, tiptoed to the communicating door and listened.

She was telephoning, talking in low, cautious tones to someone on the other end of the line. And that someone seemed in quite a temper, to judge from the cooing expla-

31

nations, the drooling promise which the girl was making.

Paul Pry smiled, walked back to his own room, turned out the lights, pulled back the bed covers, took off his shoes, yawned, stretched.

In the other room Maude the Musher had finished her telephoning, and was listening, her ear to the door, her eyes gleaming with vengeful blood lust that made them almost luminous in the darkness.

She heard the creak of the bedsprings as a tired man flung himself upon them. A little later there came the sound of rhythmic snores. Maude the Musher smiled, a smile that was utterly inscrutable. Slowly, deliberately she began to remove her clothes. The communicating door was locked only from her side.

But it was not until nearly three o'clock in the morning that she slowly turned the knob and pushed the door back upon noiseless hinges. Softly she walked into the room.

The light which seeped through the window made of her silk sheer night garment a billowy aura which served to mist the outline of her form without concealing it. She slowly made her way toward the bed, her eyes on the bulged covers.

When she came closer she started to croon.

"Dearest, you risked your life for me. Please don't think me ungrateful. I would do anything for you, anything to get you what you deserve, you—"

And, having tiptoed to within springing distance, she drew a gleaming knife from behind her back, made a leap, and finished the sentence with a burst of foul profanity which accompanied the plunging knife.

For a long moment she straddled the hump in the bed, smothering it in an embrace of death, just as a midnight owl smothers the fugitive mouse with his enfolding wings.

Then the girl jumped back with an oath of surprise. She ripped away the bedcovers.

There was nothing beneath them but a wadded blanket or two and a pillow. The knife had ripped its way into the pillow, and white feathers were sifting over the bed, drifting through the air.

"Stop That Woman!"

Paul Pry sat in his apartment, his brows level in concentration. In his hand he held a typewritten copy of a notice which had evidently been prepared and delivered by the Gilvray gang. Pry had taken it from Chick Bender's wallet.

It related to the arrival of a messenger from a large corporation that had sold an entire bond issue of three hundred and fifty thousand dollars to a local banking concern.

The corporation, it seemed, having issued the bonds in small denominational amounts, having made each one negotiable upon the theory that the issue would find its way into the hands of the small investor, now found that a bank was willing to take the entire amount.

A special messenger, carrying the three hundred and fifty thousand dollars in negotiable bonds, was due to arrive at the Union Depot the next evening at precisely 6:13.

The typewritten instructions showed the

utter thoroughness with which the organization of Big Front Gilvray functioned. Not only had all of the facts concerning the shipment of bonds been ascertained, but the spies of the organization had even gone so far as to secure a picture of the messenger.

A copy of that picture was appended to the typewritten statement. It showed a youngish man with alert eyes, a small mouth, and hair that was slicked back in the polished symmetry of perfumed splendor.

But the typewritten statement confined itself to a description of the young man and the suitcase. It said nothing concerning a *modus operandi* by which the bonds were to be transferred from messenger to gangster.

And Paul Pry was particularly interested in that. For, as has been mentioned, Paul Pry, dapper, debonaire, very fast on his feet, lived entirely by his wits. His living was, strictly speaking, within the law, for he specialized upon the recovery of stolen property for a reward.

The grand total of those rewards during the past twelve months had run into a very pretty figure. And the fact that Big Front Gilvray had been the indirect means of collecting these rewards had caused Paul Pry to regard the "big shot" as the goose who laid his golden eggs, had caused Gilvray to regard Paul Pry as a young man who must be placed upon a hot spot.

So Paul Pry sat and studied the typewritten statement through the calm, still hours of the night. He had certain facts to work upon, and only certain facts.

Maude the Musher, with her penchant for underclothed rescues, was in town. Her man, Charley the Checker, was running the checking stand at the Union Depot. The purchase of that checking stand must have cost a pretty penny, and, in view of the discovery that a young man was bringing three hundred and fifty thousand dollars in negotiable bonds at 6:13 in the evening to the Union Depot, that purchase seemed significant.

Paul Pry smoked several cigarettes over the problem. At the end of that time he went to bed. The solution seemed just out of his mental reach, like a dangling Hallowe'en apple. It was hardly likely that a young man would check a suitcase with three hundred and fifty thousand dollars in bonds at a checking station. On the other hand, it was hardly possible that the gang of Big Front Gilvray would have become interested in that checking station unless it were to be more or less intimately associated with the suitcase containing the bonds.

In the end, Paul Pry drifted off to sleep, determined to play cards as they came to his hand without worrying too much in advance about what plans or what cards the other man might hold. Which is, after all, a pretty good way to gamble, or to live.

The 6:13 Cannonball Express rumbled into the Union Depot exactly on time to the minute. The exit lane for passengers was lined with those who came to meet incoming friends, relatives or sweethearts.

Paul Pry was ensconced atop a girder where he was apparently inspecting a chipped place in the marble pillar. He wore white overalls, held a small trowel in his hand, and was utterly ignored by the stream of human traffic which milled beneath him.

The first of the passengers from the 6:13 began to arrive.

An athletic man, his face beaming in anticipation, strode through the gates, looked at the lined faces of those who waited in parallel rows. A young woman thrust her way out into the passageway. He uttered a choked exclamation, and they clinched each other tightly.

About them swirled other passengers. Groups were formed and swept about. Red-capped porters pushed carts loaded with stacked baggage.

Paul Pry kept his eyes upon the athletic-looking young man who had been the first up the exit lane. For the girl who had met him with such wild affection, who had brought that choked exclamation to his eager lips, was none other than Maude Ambrose, from Chicago, known as Maude the Musher.

She was attired in a fur coat which came a trifle below her knees, yet did not interfere with a vision of silken contours which stretched smoothly from ankle to knee.

They were within a few feet of the checking stand where the gangster known as Charley the Checker, a purple welt across his forehead, his eyes a little cloudy with the after-effects of a concussion, solicited travelers to deposit their suitcases.

Directly behind Charley the Checker, within three feet of the brass-topped counter along which suitcases were slid by those desiring to check them, was a shelf upon which some three dozen suitcases were stacked, side by side. They were each placed on end, their handles to the front, and pasteboard checks dangled from those handles.

Paul Pry noticed that there was one vacant space almost in the center of those suitcases. He watched and waited.

Two men were shaking hands profusely within a few inches of Maude the Musher and her new-found boy friend. A slender chap with cautious eyes and a cleft in his chin, pushed his way through the crowd. His right hand held the handle of a suitcase in a grip that was so tight the skin showed a dead white over the clenched knuckles.

Maude the Musher stepped back from the embrace of the young man. He made a playful grab at her, caught the sleeve of her fur coat. Maude the Musher jerked back.

The fur coat slid from her smoothly polished figure, and the crowded passengers and spectators became rooted to the spot.

There have been rumors of young women who, dressing hurriedly or carelessly for the street, have contented themselves with throwing a fur coat over filmy underthings, donning shoes and stockings and going demurely about their business.

But now the spectators had an opportunity to see for themselves that these rumors were not without their foundation.

Maude the Musher stood in such a position that the curves of her figure showed to the best advantage. The fur coat was on the tiled floor before her. Her pink silken undies were the latest mode, and had the most expensive ornamentation.

And, as though to direct all eyes to her, she screamed.

The traveling public have grown accustomed to colored photographs of beauties in underthings upon the advertising pages of the women's magazines. They have seen sights in Pullman cars, and, perhaps through hotel windows, that have made the colored photographs seem rather pale. But the sight of a woman in the flesh, clad as Maude the Musher was clad, was enough to root every one in his tracks for a swift instant.

Maude the Musher, after that scream, doubled forward and reached for the fur coat. A man sprang forward to assist her.

Someone was knocked scrambling in that mad rush, and that someone was the youth who was carrying the suitcase in so tight a grip.

In falling he seemed to hit his head. For

he lay still, limp. Only Paul Pry's watching eyes had seen the hissing slungshot. All other eyes had been fastened upon Maude the Musher and the man who was springing to her assistance.

Only the eyes of Paul Pry, of all those spectators, saw exactly what happened to the suitcase which the young man had been carrying. For that suitcase was juggled with the well-trained coordination of a football squad sending the ball into an intricate play.

The suitcase was handed to one of the men who had been shaking hands. That man handed back a similar suitcase, and that similar suitcase sprawled on the floor so that it skidded directly against the prostrate form of the young man.

The suitcase the young man had been carrying passed through the hands of two people and thudded upon the brass-covered counter of the checking stand. Charley the Checker moved with lightning like rapidity. He flipped the suitcase into the vacant space on the shelf, turned his back and faded from sight.

After all, being a known gangster has its disadvantages, and Charley the Checker knew that for the police to recognize him as the man in charge of the checking station might be exceedingly embarrassing. But he could trust no other with the delicate problem of handling the stolen bag.

After the hue and cry should die away, those securities would find their way into financial channels through sources which were divers and devious, yet none the less available.

But, the theft accomplished without a hitch, Charley the Checker "ducked out" and his place was taken by a slender man with very pale skin, but with eyes that were as cold as those of a rattlesnake.

Maude the Musher grabbed her fur coat about her and ran. Someone laughed. A traveling man dropped his suitcase to clap his hands in applause, and half a dozen laughing males joined in the applause. A policeman grinned broadly and shouldered his way through the crowd.

"Keep movin'," he said, good-naturedly, and then saw the sprawled figure of the young man with the cleft chin. Two sympathetic passengers from the train were picking him up.

The officer thought with chain-lightning efficiency. He blew his whistle, raised his voice.

"Stop that woman!" he yelled.

And the crowd, sensing that all was not as it should have been with Maude the Musher, took up the cry. There was a car waiting at the curb with motor running. The athletic young man unburdened by any baggage, gained this car, jumped behind the wheel. Obviously, it had been left there for that very purpose. Maude the Musher, her running handicapped somewhat by the neccessity of keeping the fur about her, was a stride or two later.

But she very wisely rid herself of her impedimenta by tossing the fur coat at the machine, and vaulted into the seat with a flash of well-formed limbs, a glimpse of rounded flesh.

The car was already in motion.

Police whistles shrilled. A traffic officer started tugging at his gun. The automobile violated the traffic rules, saw a hole in the oncoming lie of vehicles, and turned to the left with a great screeching of tires. The rushing land of automobiles closed up the opening, and the car was gone.

The young man with the cleft chin sat up. His eyes were completely glazed. It seemed impossible that he could know what he was doing, but he grasped for the suitcase on the floor beside him, snapped back the catch.

The suitcase was filled with those slips of tinted paper which represent waste cuttings from a printer's shop, and the young man with the cleft chin raised his voice in an agonized scream.

"I've been robbed!" he shouted. "My suitcase! Three hundred and fifty thousand dollars—"

His voice trailed off into a wail, and he slumped back, unconscious once more.

Men ran about aimlessly. The uniformed police threw a cordon about the depot. Near-by traffic officers left their posts. A hurry call brought a squad of reinforcements on the double-quick.

But the police were unable to apprehend the men responsible for the robbery. The young man with the cleft chin regained consciousness. He had remembered the spectacle of the young woman with the fur coat and the pink silk undergarments. Then someone had jostled him, there had been a terrific jar upon his head and he had dropped to the floor.

He had not even seen the faces of those who had been responsible. The blow with the slungshot had come from behind, and that which followed had been done with such well-trained efficiency as to baffle detection.

Paul Pry sat upon his post, listened to all that followed. From time to time, his eyes dropped to the check stand where the pale-faced man took in suitcases and gave them out. And all the time the suitcase with its contents of bonds reposed back of the counter.

It was, as yet, too hot to handle. And what better hiding place could be devised for it than to have it nestled in amongst some two dozen other bags staring the police in the face?

—5—

Slick and Clean

Paul Pry fastened a bit of cement to the marble, repaired the chipped place, climbed down and took a street car. He didn't go far, however.

There were stores near the depot that specialized in needs for the traveler. Cheap suitcases, made up to imitate expensive baggage, were displayed in windows with temptingly low prices placarded upon them.

Paul Pry became a customer of one of these stores, and his purchases were most peculiar.

He negotiated for a suitcase, two alarm clocks, a set of dry batteries, some junk radio equipment which loomed imposingly as a mass of tangled, coiled wires, sockets, polished metal, yet which was worth virtually nothing.

The proprietor was rubbing his hands when Paul Pry left.

Paul Pry secured a taxicab, wound up the alarm clocks, placed them inside the suitcase together with his other purchases, set the alarms on the clocks with extreme care, and ordered the cab driver to take him to the Union Depot.

He arrived at a time when trains were leaving and pulling in, when night traffic to the city was just commencing.

There was a vehicle cordon of police about the place, but they were scrutinizing suitcases that went out rather than suitcases that came in, and Paul Pry called a red cap.

"Take this to the checking stand and get me a check on it," he said.

The porter moved off with the suitcase,

and any noise which might have been made by the noisy ticking of the clocks was entirely drowned out in the tramp of feet, the roar of trains, the blare of automobile horns.

The porter returned with a slip of pasteboard bearing a number, received a generous tip, and promptly forgot about the entire matter. Paul Pry drove to his apartment, changed his clothes, ignored the pessimistic comments of Mugs Magoo, and returned to the Union Depot.

This time he carried a cane, rather a long, slender cane with a hook in the handle. He moved with the alert caution of a cat.

A glance showed him that the suitcase he desired was still in its place. That place was of advantage to the gangster who had flipped it there, because it required only a single sweeping motion with his right arm to transfer it there from the brass-covered counter.

Paul Pry took in the situation with calculating eye, and bided his time.

That time came when the evening trains had pulled out, when comparative silence descended upon the Union Depot. There were still hurrying throngs, but they were swallowed in the vast space of the huge terminal as though they had been but a handful of passing pedestrians.

Sounds became more audible.

Paul Pry looked at his watch, strolled to the curb, summoned a cab, had the driver wait for him.

"I'll be out in a few minutes. Got to meet the wife on one train and sprint across the city to make a connection at the other depot. She's bringing me my suitcase. Came away without it this afternoon. You be all ready to go as soon as I get here."

The cab driver nodded, yawned, pocketed a tip.

"I'll get you there," he promised.

Paul Pry strolled back to the station, went to the battery of public telephone booths. Through the glass door of the booth he selected he could see the pasty-faced man on duty at the checking stand.

He was, doubtless, such a man as had no readily available police record. Yet he would hesitate to appeal to the police for protection in an emergency.

Paul Pry deposited a coin and gave the number of the telephone at the checking stand. He saw the pasty-faced man scoop up the telephone to his ear, answer it. Over the wire, to his ear, came the sound of a mechanical voice.

"Yeah, hello. This is the checkin' ag'ncy Un'n Depot."

Paul Pry let his voice rasp in raucous warning.

"I'm going to blow up the whole Union Depot," he said. "There's a blast going off in exactly three minutes. I want to wreck the building, but I don't want to kill you. I've nothing against you. What I'm fighting is Capitalism. You are just a working man."

The voice over the wire had lost its mechanical disinterest.

"What're you talkin' about?" it demanded.

And Paul Pry could see that the features of the pasty-faced man had become rigid with alarm

"I've got a bomb planted. It's in a suitcase I checked with you this afternoon. There are two alarm clocks in it. The first one will go off in five minutes. Then there will be an interval of five minutes and the second one will go off. When that second one goes off it'll set loose the explosion which will wreck . . ."

That was as far as he got, for the pasty-faced man had dropped the telephone and was sprinting for the back of the checking stand where long shelves furnished storage space for suitcases.

The first alarm had gone off, and the pasty-faced man was taking no chances.

Paul Pry darted from the booth, walked swiftly to the brass-covered counter, reached out with his cane. The hooked handle slid through the curved grip of the suitcase he wanted. A jerk, and it came from the shelf, went through the air and lit fairly upon the brass-covered counter.

The pasty-faced man was no coward. He had pulled down the suitcase Paul Pry had "planted" earlier in the evening, had cut loose the leatheroid side, and was pulling out the miscellaneous assortment of wires and clocks.

His back was, of necessity toward the counter during those few brief seconds while he worked.

Paul Pry took the suitcase, strolled casually toward the taxicab exit. The cabbie ran forward and grabbed the suitcase. Paul Pry stepped into the waiting cab and was whisked away.

Inspector Oakley twisted his cigar from one side of his mouth to the other.

"You've been collecting a lot of rewards lately," he said to Paul Pry.

That individual nodded cheerfully.

"After a fifty-fifty split with you, inspector."

Oakley studied the tip of his smoldering cigar.

"Well, I guess it's all right, only you're sure going to be on a hot spot one of these days. Gilvray's gunning for you—but that's no news to you. Do you know, Pry, I have a hunch that if you'd go before the grand jury and testify to some of the things you know about Gilvray and his methods, you could get an indictment that would stick."

Paul Pry smiled.

"And why should I do that, inspector?"

"It would bust up his gang, relieve you of the certain death that's hanging over your head."

Paul Pry laughed outright.

"And kill the goosie that lays such delightful golden eggs for me—for us! Oh, no, inspector. I couldn't think of it. By the way, inspector, I understand the corporation that lost the bonds has offered twenty thousand dollars for their return. Is that right?"

Oakley grunted.

"Yeah. They'll probably be stuck for the

whole issue if they don't get 'em back, but they're so tight they only offer twenty thousand. Maybe there's a legal question about delivery. I don't know. I understand the lawyers are in a snarl over it. It seems that if the messenger who was robbed was a messenger of the bank that's buying the bonds there was a delivery and the bonds, being negotiable, can be cashed as against the company. If the messenger was in the employ of the company there wasn't any delivery, or some such thing. It's too fine spun for me."

Paul Pry extended a tapering hand, held his cigarette over the ash tray, flipped off the ash with a little finger that gave just the right thrust to drop the ashes in a pile in the center of the tray.

"Suppose we split that reward fifty-fifty?"

Inspector Oakley's cigar sagged as his lower jaw dropped in surprise.

"You've got 'em?"

"Oh no. I wouldn't have them, but my underground intelligence department advises me that the suitcase containing them has been checked in a certain checking stand in one of the large department stores here in the city.

"I could advise you of the name of that store. I might even advise you of the number of the check. Then you could recover the bonds, announce that the police had 'acted upon a tip received from the underworld through the lips of a stool pigeon, swooped down and recovered the bonds, and the culprit had escaped.' Of course, you could take considerable credit—and ten thousand dollars in cold cash. That's rather a pretty addition to the pile of reward money you've been collecting.

"Naturally, I'd want my name kept out of it. It wouldn't do to have the bulk of the police force watching me with suspicion."

Inspector Oakley took a deep breath. His eyes glittered with avarice.

"This is something like! A nice clean job. I could pull that without having so damned many questions asked. Getting some of the swag you've tipped me off to has looked pretty raw and I've had to make a pay-off on some of my reward split; but this is slick and clean."

Paul Pry smiled.

"Yes, inspector, you're right. This is slick and clean. The location of the suitcase will be telephoned to you anonymously at precisely three minutes after midnight tonight. You can still make the morning papers with it."

"Why at three minutes after midnight?" asked Inspector Oakley.

"So that you can have a witness or two present to verify your statement that the information was telephoned in from an undercover man or a stool pigeon, as you may prefer to make the explanation."

Inspector Oakley shook hands.

Benjamin Franklin Gilvray occupied rather a pretentious dwelling in the more or less exclusive residential district. A well-kept lawn surrounded his house. The arch-gangster found that it was well to keep up a front, particularly during these troubled times when so many of his deals went sour.

He lay in his soft bed, covered by blankets of the most virgin wool, his pillow a mass of wrinkles where he had been tossing around and turning during the night. The morning sun was seeping in through the windows.

Big Front Gilvray had not slept well.

A hoarse combination of sound came from the front of the house. He waited for silence, tried to doze off again, but the sound was repeated.

54

He arose angrily, and flung up the curtain.

What the hell was the matter with the boys that they let things like this happen? They knew he wanted silence.

He looked out into the pale sunlight and saw a goose, tethered with a string to a peg driven in the lawn. The goose was strutting about with a neck crooked in suspicious uncertainty, a chest thrown well out, and a tail that wiggled from side to side with every web-footed stride.

To the neck of the goose was attached a metal band and from this band dangled a piece of paper.

Big Front Gilvray sounded the alarm.

Two choppers swung machine guns into place. The goose might or might not be a trap. He might carry an infernal machine for all they knew. The machine guns cut loose.

Bits of sod and dirt flew up from the lawn about the tethered goose. Then, as the guns centered, there was a burst of feathers, and the bird dropped into a limp heap.

Covered by one of the machine guns, a gangster sprinted out on the lawn, retrieved the dead bird, brought it into the house.

It was an ordinary goose. About its neck,

attached to the metal band, was a bit of paper upon which was the message Big Front Gilvray had come to hate with a bitter hatred that transformed him from man to savage.

DEAR GOOSIE. THANKS FOR ANOTHER GOLDEN EGG.

The message was signed with two initials—P. P.

And the morning paper which reposed on the front porch of the big mansion carried screaming headlines announcing that Inspector Oakley would collect a twenty thousand dollar reward for the recovery of a third of a million dollars in negotiable bonds.

Big Front Gilvray, his anger transcending the bounds of sanity, grabbed the torn, bloody carcass of the bird and flung it across the room. It thudded to the wall with a splash of red, and a fluttering shower of feathers drifted through the room.

Big Front Gilvray tore the paper into small bits and stamped upon them. His gangsters looked at one another in consternation. The chief was usually so suavely certain of himself that to see him like this caused them to lose confidence and respect.

"Get that damned dude. Get him on the spot!" yelled Big Front Gilvray.

But Paul Pry, peacefully sleeping, assured that his bank account would be augmented by another ten thousand dollars, was beyond being troubled by the rumbled threats of the gangster.

As Inspector Oakley had so aptly remarked, the deal was "slick and clean."

Hell's Danger Signal

Against gangdom's slickest pair "Mugs" Magoo had warned him, yet deliberately Paul Pry had laid his plans. Did he have nine lives, nine charmed lives that he dared disregard all warning—dared overstep hell's danger signal unafraid?

Paul Pry noticed that the street seemed strangely deserted, and attributed the fact to a mere temporary lull in traffic.

He glanced at the opposite sidewalk where "Mugs" Magoo, ex-camera-eye man for the metropolitan police, was crouched against the wall of a bank building.

Mugs Magoo was waving his hand in a series of slow circles. That was the signal of danger—the danger sign that Paul Pry had instructed his lieutenant was to be used only in the event circumstances necessitated a hasty retreat.

It would, of course, have been the part of wisdom to have heeded that signal, for Mugs Magoo knew the underworld as perhaps no other living mortal. For years he had been on the force, merely tabulating crooks, filing their faces away in that card index memory of his. Then a political upheaval had lost him his job; an accident had lost him his right arm at the shoulder; and, he had become a drifter.

Right at present he was taking the part of a cripple, selling pencils. His hat, half filled with pencils, and with just a few coins in the bottom, was balanced on the palm of his left hand. His face was covered with a two day's growth of grayish stubble, and his glassy eyes seemed utterly uninterested in life.

But, as a matter of fact, Mugs Magoo catalogued the underworld as it flowed past, on the side street that was to the gangster what Wall Street was to the financier. And Mugs' hand, making signals with the hat, checked off the gangsters as they passed and relayed the information to Paul Pry.

The danger signals increased in intensity.

But Paul Pry was curious. His eyes were diamond hard, and there was a taut alertness about his well-knit figure that showed he had seen and interpreted the signal. Otherwise he might have been merely a well-dressed lounger, idling away the late evening on the city's streets.

A big car rolled around the corner, purred smoothly to the curb, on the same side as that occupied by Paul Pry. The door opened, and a woman stepped to the pavement.

Paul Pry made his living by his wits. He loved excitement, and he had no mental perspective when it came to courting danger. Lately he had made his money, and a very great deal of money, through the simple process of shaking down gangsters, matching his wits against their brute force.

And Paul Pry had learned from bitter experience that gangsters are very resentful indeed, and wont to show their resentment with pellets which are belched from a machine gun. He had also learned that beautiful women are, by very virtue of their beauty, likely to prove exceedingly false and dangerous.

But none of those facts dimmed in the least Paul Pry's appreciation of beauty. Nor did the danger curb his unique activities. So far, his agile wits had always kept him at least one jump ahead of those gangsters who wanted to remove him from the trials and tribulations of an unkind, but very interesting world.

This woman was particularly beautiful. But her beauty had a suggestion of smooth hardness about it, like the polished surface of a diamond. She was clad in evening gown and a white fur coat that should have made her seem like a pure snowflake. In reality, she resembled an icicle, glitteringly hard and utterly cold, despite the beautiful figure, the graceful curve of the chin, and the profile which might have been chiseled from the finest marble by the most skilled artist.

Paul Pry let his eyes slither over to the shadows across the street where Mugs Magoo crouched in watchful waiting.

Mugs had ceased to move his hat. The danger sign was discontinued. Either the danger had passed, or else it was too late for a warning to do any good.

The woman stared at Paul Pry, and there was nothing of virginal innocence in that stare. On the other hand, it was not the stare of one who wishes to make an acquaintance. It was merely that she wished to look at Paul Pry for reasons of her own, and she looked at him without seeking to disguise the fact.

The woman was hardly the type to drive an automobile. Her expensive clothes, the pride of her bearing, created an impression of surroundings that should have included a liveried chauffeur, a big limousine, an expensive apartment.

Yet she had been the one who had piloted the car, and the car was not a limousine. It was big and powerful, but was an open touring car with side curtains, partially concealing the back.

The woman's eyes glittered over the face of Paul Pry. Then she relaxed. A certain tension which had held her rigid seemed to have dissolved. The look of hardness vanished from her face. She became a creature of softly seductive curves, of ravishing beauty, and she moved toward the door which was at the rear of the touring car with the grace of a professional dancer crossing the stage.

Her arm shot out. The gloved hand opened the door. The interior of the car seemed empty.

"O.K., Bill," she said.

The plush robe on the floor of the car stirred into life. A casual observer would, perhaps, have expected some huge dog to answer the call and emerge from beneath the lap robe.

But it was no dog that shook off the folds of the robe and came out into the tang of the night air.

It was a man.

The man wore evening clothes. Someone had smashed a terrific blow on his nose; the eyes were swollen; the front of the starched shirt and the waistcoat showed plainly the stains of crimson which had spouted from the nose.

The coat was ripped. A pocket had been literally torn out, and was dangling from the threads which bound the bottom of the pocket to the coat. One of the silk lapels was ripped half away. There was no hat. The hair was matted, and the swollen nose made breathing through the mouth a necessity.

He was undignified as he crawled out of the shelter of the robe, staggered to the pavement. The woman extended a solicitous hand to his arm.

What followed came with that overlapping swiftness of events which is as impossible to follow in detail as the well-organized offensive of a well-drilled football team, sweeping down the field in a bewildering change of positions, executed at top speed.

Doorways opened, and men came out of the darkness, running low. The street lights glinted from the steel weapons. Yet no shots were fired.

One of the men swung a swift arm, and the blackjack "kerthunked" on the matted hair of the individual who had already seen such rough usage.

Another man jumped behind him, was ready to receive the unconscious form as it slumped backward and down.

Another swung a vicious blackjack at the woman's head. She, too, would have been unconscious but for one thing, and that one thing was Paul Pry.

Paul Pry carried a cane, which, to the casual eye, was merely a polished bit of wood. Only the trained observer would have noticed that that which seemed to be wood was not wood at all, but steel painted to resemble polished wood. That steel was very thin, and furnished the sheath for a tempered blade of finest steel which was attached to the handle of the cane.

It was, in the hands of a trained fencer, a highly efficient weapon, and Paul Pry was adept in its use. His right hand jerked out the naked steel of the blade.

The lights glinted from it as it darted forward, as smoothly rapid as the tongue of a snake. The man who was swinging the blackjack at the woman's skull jumped back with a scream. The cold steel had flicked out and bit deep into the shoulder muscles. The swinging arm was deflected, and the blackjack whizzed down in a harmless swing.

A car came around the corner, driven in second gear, the tortured tires shrieking their protest as they skidded over the pavement. Two men turned with oaths to Paul Pry.

But there were no shots fired. For some reason, the assailants seemed to require absolute silence so far as their operations were concerned. It was an affair of steel and blackjacks. The glittering knives swept in wicked thrusts, and the men swung their blackjacks. But Paul Pry, standing with his left arm thrown about the woman, holding her closely to him, swung his blade in a flickering arc of deadly speed.

The steel flecked in and out forming a barrier of perfect defense, biting once in a while into the bodies of the attackers.

The woman swung. Her right hand came out from beneath the fur of the coat. There was a pearl handled, nickeled automatic smuggled in the palm.

"I'll shoot, you rats!" she blazed.

The defense was too strong. The attackers jumped back. There was a muffled command.

"He's in the car," said someone.

"O.K., boys," rasped a voice. "Leave the—"

And the epithet which he used to describe the woman was one which was usually reserved for masculine ears.

The woman broke away from Paul Pry's grasp.

"Give him back! Give him back!" she screamed.

But the figures, still moving with well-disciplined efficiency of motion, had jumped into the purring automobile which had dashed to the curb. Doors slammed. The woman's gun blazed.

The shot might have been a signal. It finished the deadly silence of the attack.

The car was ripping into grinding motion. The back wheels half spun as the power was kicked into the drive. The car seemed to jump forward, half stop, jump again.

And there were little pin pricks of fire which leaped from the darkness of that car. The street echoed to the rattle of bullets. Paul Pry felt one whip past his cheek, felt something jerk the hat from his head, heard the rattle of a leaden hail against the side of the building behind him. Then the car was away, and the firing ceased.

The woman's face was deathly white. Her crimsoned lips were wide as she stared with bulging eyes at the departing car. And then her mouth spewed curses.

Paul Pry touched her arm. "The police," he suggested.

The words affected her as would an electric shock. She jumped forward, toward the car she had driven up. One arm flung up the coat, the skirt, disclosing her shapely legs, the other pitched the weapon she had held into the back of the car, pulled open the door catch.

She raised her legs over the gear shift, slammed the feet down on the brake and clutch pedals, and she did it all with a swift efficiency, a lack of lost motion, which indicated perfect muscular coordination.

Her manner was that of one who is accustomed to swift decisions and rapid execution of those decisions. And Paul Pry, curious, sensing an opportunity to exercise his unusual talents, moving with an efficiency every whit as swiftly purposeful as that of the young woman, leaped into the seat beside her and slammed the door.

The gears were meshing by the time the door catch banged into place. Paul Pry turned his head toward the opposite side of the street as the car lurched into motion.

Mugs Magoo was crouched as he had been before the swift battle. His hat was moving in a series of circles. The danger sign. And then the car, swinging for the corner, lost Mugs Magoo from Paul Pry's vision.

——2——

The woman sent the car into hurtling speed, quested the side street, prowled about the main boulevard, and finally was forced to face the facts. She had lost the car ahead.

She slowed, turned a drawn, haggard face to Paul Pry. "He's gone!" she said.

Her voice held a note of despair, an utter hopelessness which indicated that something of the utmost importance had gone from her life.

Paul Pry nodded, his ears attuned to the throbbing of a police siren which was growing in intensity with a rapidity which betokened high speed on the part of the police car.

"I don't know how you feel about the

police," he said. "But, as far as I'm concerned—"

And his shoulders shrugged expressively as he jerked his head over his shoulder in the direction of the shrieking siren which was now drawing uncomfortably close.

The woman acted as though she had heard that siren for the first time, and her reactions were characteristically swift. She floorboarded the throttle, and the car leaped forward like a startled deer.

Paul Pry noticed that she was an expert driver as the car swung into the side street, tilted, skidded, straightened as the whirling rubber bit into the pavement, and then they went places in a hurry.

By the time the woman took her foot off the throttle for a moment, and pressed hard on the brake as a bit of traffic loomed ahead, the sound of the siren had become inaudible to Paul Pry's ears. The police car had probably gone first to the scene of the shooting.

Paul Pry grinned at the girl as the traffic signal straightened out enough to give a way through, and the young woman sent the car through that hole in the traffic like a skimming trout, snaking through an opening in some submerged logs to head for the shady shelter under an overhanging bank.

"Can I be of any assistance?" he asked.

She shook her head, and, unlike many drivers of her sex, did not turn her head as she addressed him, but kept her eyes glued to the road.

"I guess not. But you can come with me while I pour a jolt of gin into my system. God knows I need it!"

Paul Pry settled back on the cushions.

"O.K. by me," he murmured.

The car made several corners. The woman started glancing about her, swung the car in a figure eight around a space of four blocks, making certain that no one was following. Then she slammed on the brakes, switched off the lights, twisted the steering wheel, and sent the car slamming up a private driveway, midway in the block. The open doors of a narrow garage yawned ahead. The woman sent the car through those doors, skidded the tires on the floor of the garage just when it seemed she would crash out the rear end of the structure, and jumped to the floor, heedless of the expensive fur coat which flapped against greasy objects, scraped dusty wheel hubs.

She was tugging at the door of the garage, getting it closed, and she apparently had no idea that Paul Pry would help her. Evidently she had been trained in self-sufficiency and did not expect those little masculine courtesies which are so priceless to most women of youth, beauty and expensive clothes.

Paul Pry gave her a hand. The door slammed into place, and a spring lock clicked.

"We go out the other way," said the woman.

She crossed the garage, groped for a door, opened it, and stood for a moment outlined against the illumination of a courtyard, listening, peering.

Then she nodded, beckoned, and stepped out upon the cement. There was a flight of stairs, a door.

Paul Pry followed her through that door and found himself in the carpeted corridor of an apartment house. They went up a flight of stairs to a second corridor, then up another flight to the third floor. The stairs were broad and carpeted with a thickness of cushioned cloth which made them absolutely silent. The illumination was not too brilliant.

The front of the apartment showed at the end of the corridor, opening upon another street, well lit. The woman's room was at the back, near those broad, well-carpeted stairs.

She paused, fitted a latchkey to the lock, then stepped back. Her keys clinked in the pocket of the coat. The right hand was concealed beneath the glistening fur of the garment. She turned the knob with her left hand, flung open the door, waited a moment, then switched on the light.

Paul Pry noticed that she had retrieved the gun from the back seat of her car, and he had no doubt as to what her right hand held beneath the concealment of the fur coat. But the woman made no effort to draw back out of the line of possible fire, or to have Paul Pry enter the apartment first. She was self-reliant, and she had been trained in the hard school of life that teaches its pupils to take things as they come.

The lights showed an apartment, well furnished, luxurious. The soft lighting glowed invitingly upon deep chairs, upon massive tables, soft couches and rich tapestries. There was an odor of stale incense in the air, and the ash trays which were on the table were filled with cigarette ashes and cigarette butts. Aside from that, the place was an example of neat housekeeping.

She walked, cat-footed, into the apartment.

"Close the door," she said to Paul Pry, flinging the words over her shoulder without turning her head, and walking toward a door which evidently opened into a bedroom.

Here she did the same thing she had done at the door of the apartment—flinging open the door with her left hand, the right still being concealed beneath the fur coat. The bedroom was not as neat as the parlor had been. Paul Pry caught glimpses of sheer silks strewn over the bed, pink fluffy garments that were on chairs.

The woman entered the room, pulled open the door of the closet, looked in it, looked under the bed. Then she walked out, went to the kitchen, kicked open the swinging door and stepped into the room. She clicked on the light switch and thrust the gun which her right hand had held, into some receptacle which had been tailored for it in the front of her dress, well out of sight. Then she sighed—turned to Paul Pry.

"Open the ice box and get some ice and a lemon. I've got some gin, and I'll get some glasses. I'm all in. How do you feel?"

"Jake a million," said Paul Pry.

She nodded casually.

"You would," she said, and took some glasses from the little cupboard over the sink, sat them on the tiled drain board. Paul Pry opened the ice box, took out a tray of ice. He noticed that the ice box was filled with bottled goods, but that there was no trace of food in it. Evidently this woman was not strong on cooking.

The drink was mixed. They clinked glasses.

"I haven't thanked you for stopping that swing that was headed for my head—not yet," she said.

Paul Pry touched his lips to the glass.

"Don't mention it," he said.

She drained her drink in three throaty gulps, tilting back her neck, drinking with a frankness that discounted all ladylike sips of the beverage, in favor of getting it down where it would do the most good.

She sighed and reached for the bottle.

"Don't be polite," she said. "I'll be one up on you in a minute."

She fixed herself a second drink. Paul Pry's glass was still half-filled as she inclined her glass to touch the brim of his for the second time.

"Here's how," she said.

She disposed of this drink more slowly.

"Well," she observed, "let's have another one and go into the other room, and have a cigarette with it."

Paul Pry held the bottom of his glass up and drained the last of the drink.

"O.K.," he observed.

She mixed the third, and then led the way into the living room, dropped in a chair. Her fur coat was open, hanging down on either side. She propped her feet up on a vacant chair.

"Happy days," said Paul Pry.

"Here's mud in your eye. Got a match?"

Paul Pry lit her cigarette, stared pensively for a moment, and sighed again.

"I love my friends, and hate my enemies," she said.

"Meaning?" asked Paul Pry.

She turned glitteringly dangerous eyes on him.

"Meaning that I hate a sniveling hypocrite," she said, "and meaning that you're a total stranger to me."

"I don't get the connection," said Paul Pry.

Her cheeks had color now, and the eyes held a moist glitter which came from the alcohol of the first two drinks.

"Meaning that if anything happened and I had to choose between a friend and a total stranger, I'd stick by the friend!" she snapped.

Paul Pry nodded. "You can't be blamed for that."

"Don't blame me, then."

"I'm not."

"Maybe you will."

"Perhaps."

There was silence for a moment.

"But," said Paul Pry, his eyes lazily regarding the smoke which curled upward from his cigarette, "it must be quite a privilege to be a friend of yours."

"It is," she agreed. There was a dreamy, reminiscent light in her eyes, as she added softly, after a moment, "And how!"

Paul Pry grinned.

"And highly inconvenient to be an enemy of yours."

The lips straightened.

"You said something!" she replied, and her words were as close clipped as bullets.

"How does one get to be your friend? Would saving your life do the trick?"

She regarded him with sober, appraising eyes.

"Well—" she hesitated.

"Well what?"

"I'm not ungrateful," she said, slowly, "but I'm just telling you, no matter what happens, a total stranger don't stack with an old friend. You remember that, no matter what else comes up between us, and then I won't feel like a damned hypocrite if I should have to sacrifice you for a friend."

Paul Pry laughed lightly.

"Baby," he said, "I like your style."

The remark added nothing to the color of her cheeks or to the warmth of her eyes.

"Most men do," she agreed.

"Now," said Paul Pry, "tell me what it was all about."

She drew a deep breath, drained off the last of the drink in the glass, and muttered something that might have been a single explosive epithet.

"You would have to ask that," she observed, and it was as though she had picked up a switch to punish a friendly dog for some infraction of discipline, so far as her manner and tone were concerned.

Paul Pry's own eyes became just a trifle diamond hard but they remained appreciative.

"The man that was with me," she said, slowly, "was my brother."

Paul Pry nodded, and there was approval in his nod.

"I thought he would be," he said tonelessly.

The young woman snapped him a suddenly questing look, but Paul Pry's face was a mask.

"Yes," she said, "an only brother."

"What did they want him for?"

"God knows. They tried to grab him off earlier in the evening. They smashed his nose. There was a doctor where we stopped the car. He was a friend of ours. They evidently figured we'd be coming there for medical attention, and they got there first and stuck around in the shadows, waiting for us to show up.

"I rather had a hunch there might be some trouble there, which is why I got out and looked things over. I spose you noticed me giving you the once-over."

Paul Pry nodded.

"And what will they do with him? Take him for a ride?"

She winced at that, kicked her feet down from the chair without answering the question. She went to the door of the kitchen.

"I'm going to have another drink."

"Count me out," said Paul Pry.

She stared moodily at him, regarding the hand that held the smoking cigarette between the fingers, noticing the steady wisps of smoke which went spiraling upward. There was no sign of tremor in the hand.

"You sure got nerves!" she said, and there was genuine admiration in her tone. "I wish," she went on, "that you wasn't—"

"Wasn't what?" asked Paul Pry.

"A total stranger," she said.

"Oh, well, it's not a permanent relationship," he observed.

She nodded gloomily.

"I've just got a hunch," she said, and stopped to regard him with pursed lips and meditative eyes. "Did you see the faces of any of those men?"

Paul Pry saw no particular reason for being truthful.

"No," he observed. "As one total stranger to another, I can tell you that I did not. I was too excited."

She laughed, a harsh, bitter laugh.

"You've been places!" she said. And then she added an after-thought. "Let's hope you don't have things done to you," she observed, and went into the kitchen to mix the other drink.

3

There sounded a whirring of an electric door device. The girl came out of the kitchen in two swift strides. Her skin matched her fur coat in color. Her right hand was once more beneath the folds of the garment.

"Got a gun?" she asked of Paul Pry, and her tone while taut with emotion, was as casual as when she had asked him if he had a match.

"I could find one if I had to," said Paul Pry.

"You may have to," she said and strode to the door.

She flung it open.

"I'll take it standing up, whatever it is," she said, before she had seen what was in the corridor.

A young boy came forward. He was in the uniform of a messenger service, and he held forward an addressed envelope.

"Miss Lola Beeker?" he asked.

The girl extended her left hand.

"You guessed it, sonny."

His eyes took in her beauty with that breathless reverence which immaturity has for a beautiful woman, when eyes are just awakening to grace of form and face, and experience has not learned to tell that beauty of figure is, after all, but beauty of figure.

"Gee!" he said, and handed her the envelope, his wide eyes still on her face. "You don't need to give me no tip, lady. It's a pleasure!"

She ignored the breathless appreciation of her beauty with a disregard which showed she accepted such homage as a matter of course. She rewarded the boy with a smile and a pat of the hand. Paul Pry's eyes noticed the mechanical nature of the smile, the casual carelessness of the pat. The boy noticed neither.

He was still standing, wide-eyed, when the girl gently closed the door and ripped the edge off of the envelope with a hand that trembled.

She pulled out a folded bit of paper and read a typewritten message. Her eyes were brilliant and hard. Her breast rose and fell with the strain of her heavy breathing.

She folded the letter, replaced it in the envelope. She looked at Paul Pry with eyes that seemed unseeing, and walked into the bedroom.

After a few moments, Paul Pry heard her voice.

"I'm getting on some more comfortable things. Open that door, will you? The boy's waiting for an answer. Tell him the lady says yes."

Paul Pry approached the door. This time he opened it with his left hand, and his right hand was hovering around the lapels of his coat.

As had been so aptly observed by the lady herself, he was a total stranger.

The boy in uniform was waiting, standing just as he had been when the door closed. His eyes showed a stab of disappointment as they focused on Paul Pry.

"The lady," said Paul Pry, "says yes."

The boy nodded, still stood, staring.

"Gee, mister," he blurted, "you ain't her husband, are you?"

"No," said Paul Pry, "I'm a total stranger, and I'm going in just a minute or two."

The boy grinned.

"Good night, mister."

"Good night," said Paul Pry, and was careful to shoot the bolt on the lock when he had closed the door.

The woman came out of the bedroom dressed in a filmy negligee.

"This," she said, "feels more comfortable."

"It looks like a million dollars," said Paul Pry.

"You gave the boy the message?"

"Yes."

She nodded.

"That was all, wasn't it?" asked Paul Pry. "Just that the lady said yes?"

Her eyes were starry.

"Ain't that enough?"

Paul Pry turned toward his glass.

"On second thought," he remarked irrelevantly, "I think I'll have another drink myself. Can I mix you one?"

And he started toward the kitchen picking up the two glasses as he went.

"No!" she snapped, and the starry gleam had gone from her eyes, leaving them as coldly observant as were the eyes of Paul Pry.

Paul Pry mixed up the drink, taking care to make far more soda water in its content than gin, and returned to the room, the ice clinking in the glass.

The woman had flung herself on the sofa.

The negligee had fallen back from her raised bare arm which held a cigarette in a long jade and ivory holder. She was staring at Paul Pry.

"That message," she said, "was from a widowed sister. Her child's sick, and she wants me to come out and stay with her tonight. I hate the thought of nursing a sick child."

"And of telling her of the brother who was taken for a ride?" he asked.

"I shan't tell her!" snapped the figure on the couch.

"I see," he muttered, noncommittally.

"You would," she flared.

Paul Pry shot her a swifter glance. The face was as fierce as that of a tigress, and it softened instantly into a smile of invitation.

"But I want to thank you—properly, when I have the opportunity, for saving my life. When can I see you?"

"Any time."

"Well. I've had a minute of relaxation, and that's enough. I'll pack my suitcase, and get started. Tell you what—you got any friends in the city?"

The tone was anxious.

"Not a friend," said Paul Pry.

Paul Pry hesitated for an appreciable fraction of a second.

A swift smile darted about her lips.

"Oh, I know," she said. "You don't need to explain. Listen, maybe you can do something else for me. Go to the Billington Hotel and register under the name of George Inman, will you. You don't need to stay there, just take a room so you'll be registered, and so you can get mail there. If you'll do that, I'll drop you a note as soon as the child gets well."

"O.K.," said Paul Pry, his face lightening. "That'll be a swell idea. George Inman, eh?"

"George Inman," she said.

The woman kicked off the folds of the negligee, and the result was rather startling.

"And get out of here, so I can get into some street clothes. I'll drop you a note."

Paul Pry finished his drink, reached for the door knob.

"I'll be seeing you," she said.

"Toodle-loo," remarked Paul Pry after the manner of a male who has been utterly hypnotized.

"Cheerio," she cooed as the door closed.

Paul Pry, in the corridor, became swiftly cautious. He didn't go down the back stairs, the way he had come, but went to the front of the building, found an automatic elevator, entered the cage and pressed the button which took him to the lobby. He walked out, past a desk where a colored lad in a brilliant uniform sat at a telephone switchboard, and out onto the lighted street.

He walked a few steps, retraced his steps and looked at the index over the mail boxes.

The woman's name was the same as that on the letter. Lola Beeker.

Paul Pry called a cab.

The address that he gave was within half a block from the place he had been standing when the woman had debouched from the car, a vision in white.

He discharged the cab, paid the meter, and stubbed his toe as he turned back to the sidewalk. He tried to get up, but sank back with a groan. The cab driver, suddenly solicitous, jumped from the cab, came toward him.

"What is it, boss?"

"I don't know," said Paul Pry. "Something happened in my leg, a nerve or something. I can't move it."

The taxi driver straightened, peered up and down the side street.

"There's a doctor over there, about seventy-five feet or so. Think you can make it?"

Paul Pry groaned, nodded.

"I'll try," he said.

A passerby, attracted by the sprawled figure, came cautiously over. The cab driver explained. Between them, they got Paul Pry to his feet and took him along the pavement to the flat where a sign announced that Philip G. Manwright, M.D., held office hours from two to five in the afternoon on every day except Sunday.

The cab driver pressed the bell.

After some two or three tries, there sounded motion from within the house, and feet thudded along the corridor which led to the door. A light clicked on, and a man in bathrobe with hair that was mussed up and eyes that were slightly swollen with sleep, regarded them in dour appraisal.

"Doctor?" asked the cab driver.

The man nodded.

"This guy did a Brode an' busted a leg or somethin' right out in front of the joint," said the driver.

"Come in," invited Doctor Manwright.

They shuffled along the corridor, into a surgical room where an operating table occupied the center of the floor under a drop-light.

"Put him down there," said the doctor.

They stretched Paul Pry out on the table.

"Which leg?" asked the doctor.

"Right."

He passed exploring fingers over it.

"Something seemed to happen and all the strength went out of it. It's pricking like pins and needles now," said Paul Pry.

The doctor frowned, flexed the leg.

"Humph."

The cab driver grinned cheerfully at Paul Pry.

"Well," he said, "I'll run along."

"Better drive the cab up and wait," said Paul Pry.

"O.K., boss."

The two men ambled awkwardly out of the room. The doctor drew the bathrobe about him and regarded Paul Pry speculatively.

"Any peculiar feeling about the heart?" he asked.

"None," said Paul Pry.

"Notice any sudden pain just above the leg when it gave out?"

"None."

"Nervous?"

"Very. I can't sleep. I got all sorts of strange symptoms."

The doctor felt the leg again.

"I'll go get some clothes on," he announced, "and we'll give you a once-over."

"Sorry to bother you," said Paul Pry. "I'm feeling better now. The circulation seems to be coming back."

"In any pain?" asked the doctor.

"Just the pins and needles."

The doctor crossed to a cabinet, took out a bottle, poured a few drops into a glass of water.

"Drink this," he said. "I'll dress and come in again. I won't be three minutes."

"O.K.," said Paul Pry and sipped at the glass.

The doctor left the room.

Paul Pry got up and dumped the mixture down the sink, crossed on swift, silent feet into the office which was next to the surgical room, and stared at the flat-topped desk, the bookcase, the card index of files.

He opened the files. The light which came from the surgical room enabled him to pick out the letters of the index. He consulted the "B's" and pulled out a card marked "Beeker, Laura."

Then Paul Pry noticed a day book on the

desk. He opened it and consulted the current date. It appeared that, between eleven and twelve, Doctor Manwright had treated a gentleman who gave the name of Frank Jamison.

Paul Pry went to the card index, and pocketed the card of Frank Jamison. Then he went back to the surgical room and stretched out on the operating table, closing his eyes and breathing regularly.

The doctor came into the room within a few minutes, looking gravely professional. The depression had undoubtedly hit the medical business, and Paul Pry felt certain that the doctor would at least lay a foundation for a stiff charge for a night visit.

Nor was he wrong. For twenty minutes the doctor examined him. At the end of that time, there was doubt and a certain suspicion in the doctor's eyes.

"You'd better come back tomorrow afternoon. What's the name?"

"George Inman."

"Where do you live?"

"Billington Hotel."

"Age?"

"Twenty-six."

"Ever had any heart trouble, dizzy spells, rheumatism?"

Paul Pry nodded gloomily.

"I feel dizzy every once in a while," he said, "and I used to have rheumatism in my right shoulder."

The doctor sucked in a yawn.

He pulled a card from a drawer, filled it out, yawned again.

"Come tomorrow afternoon at any time between two and four. The charge for this visit is—twenty dollars."

Paul Pry produced his wallet, took out the bills, peeled off a twenty. The doctor glimpsed a couple of the hundreds and one that seemed even larger in denomination. He ceased to yawn.

"I may want to put you in a hospital for observation," he said. "It's a baffling case."

"Nothing serious?" asked Paul Pry.

"I can't tell—yet."

Paul Pry tested the leg.

"Feel all right?"

"Yes, sorta numb, but all right. I can walk."

"Go to your hotel and go to bed," said Doctor Manwright.

Paul Pry hobbled to the door. The cab driver was waiting to assist him to the cab.

"Billington Hotel," said Paul Pry.

"O.K.," said the driver.

The doctor bowed, said good morning, and closed the door. Paul Pry hobbled into the cab.

—4—

At the Billington Hotel Paul Pry registered as George Inman and was given a room.

"There's a telephone call for you," said the clerk. "The party seemed very anxious to have you call as soon as you came in."

He handed Paul Pry a number.

"O.K.," said Paul Pry.

He went to his room, tipped the bell boy, pocketed the key and went out.

"Did you call the number?" asked the clerk.

"I called it," said Paul Pry.

The clerk nodded, snapped the lock on the safe, yawned.

Paul Pry boarded a cruising cab. The address which he gave was within a block of the place where the girl had driven him into the private driveway which terminated in the mysterious garage at the rear of the apartment house of such unconventional design.

Paul Pry told the cab to wait, walked the

block, climbed a fence, and found himself in the cemented courtyard in the rear of the apartment house. He opened the back door, climbed the carpeted stairs.

He paused at the door of the girl's apartment long enough to go through the formality of pressing the button of the door signal. As he had expected, there was no answer, no sign of life from within.

Paul Pry produced a flat leather receptacle which contained some two dozen keys, chosen for general efficiency. He opened the door with the third key, boldly switched on the light and walked in.

He closed and bolted the door, lit a cigarette, hummed a little tune, and walked into the bedroom.

The young woman had left her evening clothes, crumpled into a careless wad, and thrown on the bed. She had evidently donned a plain street suit which would be inconspicuous. The white fur coat was hanging in the closet.

Paul Pry looked on the top of the dresser, frowned, prowled about the drawers, paused to consider, and then went to the closet and put his hand in the pocket of the fur coat. His face lit with a smile of satisfaction as his questing fingers closed on a folded sheet of paper. He pulled it out.

It was the typewritten note that the woman had taken from the messenger boy.

Paul Pry read it.

All right, Lola, we've got Bill Saca-noni. He goes for a ride unless we get what we want and get it in a hurry. First, we want ten grand stuck in a bag and delivered at the place we told you. Second, we want George Inman put on the spot. You've stuck up for him and shielded him long enough. We know all about him. You've got until daylight to do your stuff. Then Bill gets his. We know you can get the coin, but we want to be sure about Inman.

The note was unsigned.

Paul Pry thrust it in his pocket, paused, halfway to the door, then returned and put it back in the pocket of the fur coat. He clicked off the lights, opened the door and slipped out into the corridor.

He walked to the cab, and told the driver to take him to a certain street corner near the wholesale district. That corner was near the spot where Paul Pry maintained a secret apartment, a place where he could live and be reasonably safe from danger while he formulated his plans, rested between coups.

He discharged the cab, made certain that he was not followed, and entered the apartment. Mugs Magoo blinked glassy eyes at him.

"You still here?"

"Sure. Where'd you think I was going?"

"To keep an appointment with the undertaker."

"Not yet."

Mugs Magoo grunted, reached for the bottle of whiskey that was at his elbow.

"Not yet, but soon."

Paul Pry ignored the comment, took off his hat and light coat, sat down in a chair, and lit a cigarette.

"Why the danger signal, Mugs?"

Mugs Magoo snorted.

"Because the place was lousy with guns. I spotted 'em from across the street. They were in the shadows behind you. They weren't waiting for you, or you'd have been dead long before you got the signal. But I figured there was going to be some guns popping, and the innocent bystander usually makes the biggest target. Then again, being a witness to a gang killing ain't so nice from the standpoint of life insurance risks."

Paul Pry nodded. His voice, when he spoke, was almost dreamy.

"The girl, Mugs?"

"That was Lola Beeker. She's in with a big bottle, name of Bill Sacanoni. I think that was him that crawled outa the car an' got beat up."

Paul Pry nodded.

"Why didn't they use guns, Mugs?"

"Wanted to avoid the bulls for one thing, and wanted to muscle Bill away. They'll hold him for something. The guns had the street cleared. They started turning pedestrians away right after you slipped through. There's a gangster's doctor in the block, and I guess they was spottin' his office."

Paul Pry reached in his inside pocket and took out the cards he had purloined from the files of the gangsters' physician.

He looked at the card of Lola Beeker.

It gave her name, age, address, list of symptoms that had to do with a minor nervous complaint. The card bore a notation that Bill Sacanoni would pay the bill. The card also gave the address of Bill Sacanoni.

Paul Pry turned it under, and looked at

the card of the man who had been treated that evening, between the hours of eleven and twelve.

The name was Frank Jamison. The address was in an apartment hotel well toward the upper end of town. The card gave lists of various treatments. Once the treatment was for alcoholism. Once the treatment was for gunshot wounds, and the last treatment was for a stabbing wound in the shoulder.

Paul Pry nodded.

That would be the man who had swung the blackjack at the girl, the one who had felt the bite of Paul Pry's sword cane as it jabbed home.

"Who is Frank Jamison, Mugs?"

Mugs Magoo regarded the empty whiskey glass with judicial solemnity, reached for the bottle, and knitted his brows.

"Don't place the moniker. Maybe it's phony. Know what he looks like?"

"Five feet nine, one hundred and seventy or about that. Has a funny pointed jaw, like a battleship's bow—"

Mugs Magoo interrupted. "That places him," he said, "and I remember now he used to use the name o' Jamison. It's his middle name. Frank Jamison Kling is the full name. He's a big shot. They say he makes a specialty of musclin' people into big ransoms."

"Is he," asked Paul Pry, "likely to be the head of his gang?"

"Sure. If he was in that scuffle about the car, he's the man that was running the show."

"And likely to be the one who gets the money when it's over?"

"Sure to," grunted Mugs.

"How about George Inman?" asked Paul Pry.

Mugs Magoo lowered the whiskey glass. Surprise showed in the glassy eyes that were usually so utterly devoid of expression.

"Guy," he said, "don't tell me you're monkeyin' with that bird!"

"Why?" asked Paul Pry.

Mugs Magoo heaved a deep sigh.

"I gotta hand it to you. It's a gift, gettin' into deep water every time you start wadin'. You don't ever pick no ordinary dangers. When you start gettin' into trouble, you wade right in over your necktie.

"That bird Inman, now—Well, there's talk going around about that baby. He's one of the upper crust of gangsters, and he's playing both ends against the middle. Of course, George Inman ain't nothing but a name. It's the name this big shot uses when he's slipping over a fast one.

"He works under cover all the time, and nobody's ever been able to get a line on him. They know the name, and that's all. It's a cinch he's one of the biggest shots in town. That much they know because they got sort of a line on what Inman knows.

"There's fifteen or twenty of the big guys that'd give a neat slice of jack to learn who Inman really was. When they knew, Inman wouldn't last long. If you're monkeying around with anybody that gives the name of Inman, just gimme the money to go get myself measured for a suit of black. I'll need it before I get any fatter, anyway; and I may need it as soon as the tailor can get it fitted."

Paul Pry arose, crossed to the closet where he kept his collection of drums.

He took down a Buddhist temple drum that resembled a huge bronze bowl. This drum was merely rubbed into sound, not struck with a stick as other drums were.

Paul Pry took the leather-covered stick and started rubbing the lip of the drum. His hand moved slowly. At first there was no sound whatever. Then, as the speed of the rubbing stick increased, there sounded a low monotone of sound which filled the apartment, yet which seemed to emanate from no particular source.

"It drives me nuts," said Mugs Magoo.

Paul Pry said nothing until after the last bit of sound had died away. Then he sighed, raised his eyes to Mugs Magoo's face.

"Alcohol, Mugs, has robbed your ears of their sense of rhythm."

"If they'd only rob 'em of a sense of sound, so far as those drums are concerned, so I couldn't hear 'em, I'd be better satisfied."

Paul Pry let his eyes rest dreamily upon the drum.

"It soothes the soul, Mugs. That's why they use it as a preliminary to worship in those temples where the religion is a philosophical rite of inner meditation. It's a wonderful philosophy, Buddhism, Mugs, and the drum has a tendency to fill my mind with inner quiet, a comparative poise that's so necessary to concentration."

Mugs Magoo refilled his whiskey glass.

"Yeah," he said. "It's a great philosophy maybe. But the trouble with them Buddhists is that they don't wear no pants."

Paul Pry grinned.

"That's begging the question, Mugs."

"The hell it is," retorted Mugs Magoo, "you're goin' heathen, working your mind up to the right pitch with a lot o' boomin' drums. One o' these days you'll take to smokin' one o' these here *hookahs*, an' throwin' your pants away. I'm humorin' you now, because if you was dyin' o' pneumonia, I'd give you your last wishes. You're just the same as a dyin' man right now. And if you're monkeyin' around with a guy that goes by the name of George Inman, you're just the same as parked on a marble slab."

Paul Pry laid down the drum stick.

"I'm glad you mentioned this Inman again, Mugs. It reminds me of a telephone call I almost forgot to make."

He crossed the room to the telephone, called the number which the clerk at the Billington Hotel had given him.

"Hello," he said as a feminine voice answered, "this is George Inman, at the Billington Hotel. Was someone calling me?"

At the other end of the room there came a startled gasp, a choking exclamation that was mingled with the sputtering noise of a man who is almost strangling.

The woman's voice crisped a swift comment.

"Where are you, George dear? In your room?"

It was the voice of the woman who had worn the white fur coat.

"Yes," said Paul Pry.

"Just a minute, George, there's a friend of mine wants to speak with you. He wants to give you an important message."

There came the sounds over the wire of rustling motion, then a man's voice.

"Yeah, hello," it gruffed.

"Yes?" said Paul Pry.

"Well, listen," said the man's voice, speaking hastily. "I'm a friend of Lola's. You recognized her voice over the telephone?"

"Yes. Sure," said Paul Pry, "but I'm afraid I don't want to deal with any friend of hers. My business is with her."

"Yeah, sure it is," said the man. "But she can't get to come alone. She wanted me to give you a ring so I could explain what's happened."

"She's in a jam, and she's got to see you right away. Now you wait right there in your room. Keep the door locked. Don't open up for anyone until she gets there, and don't even answer the telephone. Get me?"

"We're coming over just as soon as we

can make a break, and we want to be sure we ain't tailed. See? Now you and Lola can go ahead with that thing just like you planned, only you gotta wait until she gets there. Here she is on the telephone."

The man relinquished the instrument. The voice of the girl who had worn the fur coat came to Paul Pry's ears.

"It's all right, George. I'll explain when we get there. Only sit right in the room. Don't open until you hear someone rap twice, then a pause, then three raps, then another pause, and then a single rap.

"That'll be me. The man with me is O.K."

"O.K.," he said, at length. "If you say it's O.K. I guess it is."

"Right over," said the woman's voice. "You stay right there until we get there."

Paul Pry hung up the receiver, turned to stare into Mugs Magoo's florid features.

"Oh, Lord!" groaned Mugs. "I thought you'd done the damndest fool things a guy could ever do—but being George Inman! That takes the cake! An' when you spilled that dope it made me swallow my drink of whiskey down the wrong side of my throat, and anything that'll make a guy do that with really good whiskey, is a public calamity.

106

"Go ahead an' play around while you've got the chance, because when you get all stretched out with a coroner's jury starin' at the doctor, while he points out the course of the bullets through the body, you won't have no kick outa life at all. Just go right ahead, guy, only shake hands with me before you go out again. I hate to see you go, but you might as well finish it up and get the suspense over with."

Paul Pry grinned.

"Mugs," he said solemnly, "I have an idea that I'm going to meet some tough gangsters. That is, Mugs, they think they're tough. But, to me, they're going to be nice little goosies, laying golden eggs."

Mugs Magoo disregarded the glass in favor of more direct action. As he removed the neck of the bottle from appreciative lips, he muttered: "An' there's a frail at the bottom of it. That's a cinch."

Paul Pry nodded. He was putting on his coat, hefting the balance of his sword cane. "Yes, Mugs, you're right again. There's a lady at the bottom of it, Mugs, a lady who says yes."

Mugs Magoo extended a solemn hand.

"You was a good pal," he said, "—while you lasted!"

5

The streets of the city held that damp cheerlessness which comes a couple of hours before dawn. They were almost deserted, and Paul Pry, anxious to escape observation, walked for three rapid blocks before he swung over to the main boulevard where he knew he could find a cab even at that hour.

His actions were not even furtive. He had a coil of light rope wound around his waist, a little handbag that contained certain articles. He was smiling, rather a fixed smile, and his eyes were diamond hard.

Paul Pry sent the cab to the address given on the purloined card as being the residence of Frank Jamison. The apartment hotel was of exactly the type he had expected.

Paul Pry entered the hotel after having paid the cab, approached the desk. He wrote his name on the register.

"Something for about a month," he said. "Frank Jamison knows me. He said I'd be comfortable here. I'd like to get on the same floor he's on. Maybe I'll be longer than a mouth. Maybe it won't be so long, but you get a month's rent cash on the nail."

The man at the desk nodded.

"Mr. Jamison's on the fourth, 438. I can let you have 431. That's just a ways down the corridor and on the other side."

"O.K.," said Paul Pry. "Jamison ain't in, is he?"

"I don't think so. He's out quite late."

"Yeah, I know. Give'm a buzz, just in case."

The man behind the counterlike desk stepped to the glassed-in partition behind which sat a telephone operator.

"Give Jamison in 438 a jingle. Tell him his friend's here, Mr. Pry."

The girl plugged in a line, shook her head, after an interval.

"Out," said the man as he swung around to face Paul Pry.

"Now listen, Frank Jamison and me are going to do some business that we ain't telling all of Frank's friends about. So when Frank comes in, he'll have some guys with him. Just don't say anything about me being here."

The clerk was businesslike.

"We make a practice of minding our own business here, Mr. Pry. You make your own announcements. And the first installment, by the way, will be one hundred dollars."

Paul Pry handed the clerk two bills.

"Never mind the receipt. I'm hitting the hay. The baggage'll get here in the morning."

Paul Pry went to the fourth floor, was shown to his apartment. He tipped the boy who took him up, waited until he heard the elevator door clang shut, and then walked down the corridor to 438, fitted his key assortment to the lock until he had the proper skeleton, heard the bolt click, and walked in. He left the hall door open, and the light from the hallway flooded enough of the room to give him the lay of the land.

Paul Pry entered the bedroom, ripped the blankets from the bed, went to the bathroom, soaked the blankets in water, wrung out some of the surplus, took the wet blankets into the front room, suspended them by their corners.

He worked with swift precision, and used the coil of light rope, hardly more than a heavy twine. He anchored this rope to the chandeliers, easing the weight of the blankets on the light rope so that he would not pull out the lighting fixture.

When he had finished, he had two wet blankets suspended in such a manner that they almost blocked the rest of the room from the doorway.

He took from his pocket a little metallic object that resembled a fountain pen, stood a little distance back from the wet blankets, pointed the metallic object, and pressed a hidden button.

There was a dull explosion, sounding hardly more loud than the smashing of a small inflated paper bag. A stream of swirling vapor mushroomed out until it hit the wet blankets. Then it seemed to be enveloped, the tear gas having an affinity for the moist surface.

Paul Pry stepped swiftly out of the apartment room, closed the door behind him, used his skeleton key, and twisted the bolt of the lock.

Then he went down the corridor, took some of the light rope, measured off the length of the corridor, and took a round door stop from the little bag which he carried. He screwed this door stop into the wood of the corridor, well over to one side, made a loop in the rope with a bowline knot holding it against slips, dropped the loop over the door stop, then screwed a similar door stop into the other side of the corridor.

When he tightened the rope, he had a

perfectly taut line some three inches above the level of the floor. He surveyed the result, nodded, removed the rope, leaving the door stops in place, and went back to his own room.

The place where he had put the door stops was almost opposite the entrance of apartment 431, the one on which he had paid the rent.

He yawned, removed his shoes, closed, but did not lock the door, lit a cigarette, and sprawled out in one of the overstuffed easy chairs.

There was the first glint of dawn in the air, although the interior of the apartment hotel still remained murked with darkness when Paul Pry consulted his wrist watch and frowned. It looked very much as though he had drawn a blank.

The slamming of the elevator door at the end of the corridor came to his ears, and his stockinged feet came to the carpeted floor of his room with swift silence. He approached the door, opened it the merest crack.

There were three men walking down the hallway with grim efficiency. One of them carried a black bag. His right shoulder was bulky with bandage.

They paused before room 438. Keys rattled.

"Anyway," husked one of the men in a low voice, "Inman was registered there. He must have—"

"Shut up," snapped one of the group.

The hoarse voice ceased abruptly.

The man who held the bag opened the door of the room.

The three barged in there.

Paul Pry stepped out of his door, tossed the loop of twine over the door stop, twisted the other end of the rope over the other door stop, stepped back in the doorway of his room. He made no effort to conceal himself. His shoes, laces knotted, were in his belt. His eyes, diamond hard, were staring down the corridor.

The door of 438 burst open. Three men spewed from the room, hands stretched outward. There was the glint of the dim light on blued steel, the sound of terror stricken oaths.

The man who had fitted the key to the lock continued to carry the bag. But there was a gun in his other hand.

They ran down the corridor with awkward steps, their streaming eyes of no use to them. Blinded, they groped and stumbled. They passed Paul Pry's door, and then hit the rope.

The first man took the second with him as he went down. The third stumbled over the heap. A gun went off with a roar, and the sound of curses followed the detonation.

Paul Pry stepped from his room.

His position could not have been chosen with better care, nor to better advantage. He held a blackjack in his hand, the leather thong looped around his wrist.

The man with the bag straightened.

The blackjacket did its stuff with smooth efficiency. Paul Pry's hand closed about the handle of the black bag as the grip of the man who had been sapped relaxed.

There sounded a woman's scream. A figure in pajamas opened one of the doors. Another shot rang out. The man in pajamas jumped back for the shelter of his room.

Paul Pry walked down the hall toward the back stairs. His stockinged feet gave no sound. As he reached the stairs, he slipped his shoes on, and ran down the staircase.

Day was dawning as he slipped the chain on a side exit and walked out into the street.

The street was calm with the gray tranquility of early dawn.

Paul Pry walked swiftly, slowed his pace when he was well away from the building, picked up a cab after he had been walking for about ten minutes. He gave the address of a downtown hotel, and was taken there at top speed.

He discharged the cab, broke his trail by going to the Union Depot in another cab and taking a third cab to his apartment.

Mugs Magoo was asleep, sprawled in the easy chair, his relaxed hand stretched toward the whiskey bottle. The bottle was empty.

Paul Pry grinned, closed the door, locked it, turned his attention to the bag. It was locked. He took his knife and slit it open.

The interior, back of where the leather bulged out through the cut edge, showed a mass of greenbacks.

"There should be ten grand here," said Paul Pry.

He chuckled softly as he counted it and found that it was an even ten thousand dollars.

He took the bag and the money, crossed to the safe, opened the fireproof receptacle, tossed in bag and money, closed the door, spun the dial of the combination, and went to bed.

Past experience had taught him that Mugs Magoo desired nothing more than to be left alone. He would awaken presently, seek the water tap and then go to bed. In the morning he would be as glassily-eyed efficient as ever.

Paul Pry slept the morning through.

The afternoon shadows were creeping across the street, when he felt a hand at his shoulder.

He looked up into the puzzled countenance of Mugs Magoo.

"Listen, guy," said Mugs, "I don't want to disturb your beauty sleep, but there's a lot o' stuff goin' on, an' I'm afraid it's something that you're concerned about."

Paul Pry grinned the sleep out of his eyes, and ran his fingers through tousled hair.

"Shoot," he commented, briefly.

"It's about Inman and Lola Beeker, and this guy, Sacanoni," said Mugs Magoo, speaking rapidly, and out of one side of his mouth. "It seems Jamison got Sacanoni, and used the muscle stuff to make Lola Beeker get ten grand that they'd put away for getaway money in case anything happened.

"Then it seems Lola Beeker knew who this guy Inman really was. They made her turn him up. But she worked some sort of a funny gag, and Inman slipped out of his room in the hotel with the whole damned place literally swarming with gunmen.

"But they let Sacanoni go when the Jane kicked through with her share of the info and the ten grand. Then Beeker and Sacanoni did a fade."

Paul Pry yawned.

"But," he said, "why wake me up?"

"Because," said Mugs, "there's a late tip out that this Inman that's been raising so much hell was really Sacanoni all the time. The gangs knew that Lola Beeker knew who Inman was, but they never figured he might be just another name for Sacanoni. So, then, who was this guy at the Billington Hotel?"

Paul Pry reached for the cigarettes.

"Mugs," he observed, "you still haven't any reason for disturbing *my* slumbers."

Mugs Magoo blurted out that which came next.

"The hell I haven't. Listen to this. When Jamison and his gang went to salt the ten grand something happened and they got slicked out of it. They thought it was this guy, Inman, only—"

"Only what?" asked Paul Pry.

"Only they found that some guy had come in and taken a room right where it'd do the most good, and that this bird registered under the name of Paul Pry! And there's ten thousand berries gone bye-bye."

Paul Pry grinned.

"Mugs," he said, "you misjudge me. All I did was to deliver a message. I delivered it to a boy. I simply told him 'The lady says yes,' and that was all."

Mugs nodded solemnly.

"But there's ten grand in the safe this morning."

Paul Pry let his face brighten.

"Maybe. Mugs, while we were both asleep, a dear little goose came and laid another golden egg!"

Dressed to Kill

"I'll see that the undertaker gives you the breaks when it comes to the music," said "Mugs" Magoo as Paul Pry started out. For he knew his friend was about to dance with death. Pry's very costume was enough to turn any fancy-dress ball into a murder masquerade.

1

The Smuggled Letter

Looking very uncomfortable in his evening clothes, "Mugs" Magoo rolled his glassy eyes and nodded across the table to Paul Pry.

"The place is full of crooks," he said.

Paul Pry, the very opposite in appearance of his companion, wore evening clothes as though they had been molded to fit him. He looked at Mugs Magoo with eyes that glittered with attention.

"What sort of crooks, Mugs?" he asked.

"Well," said Magoo, "it's a funny set-up. I've got a hunch if you knew what was going on here tonight, you'd know where the Legget diamond is."

"What do you mean, Mugs?"

Mugs Magoo gestured with a fork. "That guy over there," he said, "is Tom Meek."

"All right," Paul Pry said, "who's Tom Meek?"

"A letter smuggler."

"A letter smuggler, Mugs?" asked Paul Pry. "I never heard of such a thing."

Mugs Magoo manipulated his fork so as to get a mouthful of food. His right arm was off at the shoulder and his left hand had to do the work of both cutting and conveying food while he was eating, gesticulating while he was talking.

"Tom Meek," he said, "smuggles letters out of the jail. That's where he picks up his side money."

"He's a jailer?" asked Paul Pry.

"Yeah, sort of a deputy, third-assistant jailer. He's hung around the jail through three administrations. He smuggles letters out for prisoners."

Paul Pry nodded and filed the information away for what it might be worth. His keen eyes stared at the man Mugs had indicated. A small inconspicuous individual, with gray hair, high cheek bones and watery eyes.

"Looks harmless, Mugs," said Paul Pry.

Mugs Magoo nodded casually. "Yeah," he said, "he don't do anything except smuggle letters. That's his racket. He won't touch anything else. He won't even take hop in to the prisoners."

"All right," persisted Paul Pry, "why do

you think that Tom Meek, the letter smuggler, knows anything about the Legget diamond?"

"He don't," Mugs Magoo agreed readily enough. "But you see that heavy-set fellow over there at the table, with the jaw that's the blue-black, in spite of the fact he's been shaved not over two hours ago, the guy with the black hair and the big chest?"

"Yes," said Paul Pry, "he looks like a lawyer."

"He is a lawyer. That's Frank Bostwick, the criminal lawyer, and he's attorney for George Tompkins, and Tompkins is the man that's in jail for pulling the robbery that netted the Legget diamond."

"All right," said Paul Pry, "go on, Mugs."

Mugs swung his head in the other direction. "And the tall dignified coot over there with the starched collar and the glasses is Edgar Patten, and Patten's the confidential representative of the insurance company that had the Legget diamond insured."

Paul Pry watched Mugs Magoo thoughtfully, his eyes glittering with interest despite their preoccupation.

"Well, Mugs," he said, "give me the lowdown on it and perhaps I can turn the information to some advantage."

Paul Pry lived by his wits alone. He would have indignantly denied that he was a detective in any sense of the word; on the other hand, he could have demonstrated that he was not a crook. Had he been called upon to give his business, he might have described himself as a professional opportunist.

Mugs Magoo, on the other hand, had a definite status. He was confidential adviser to Paul Pry.

Mugs never forgot a name, a face, or a connection. At one time he had been "camera-eye" man on the metropolitan police force. A political shake-up had thrown him out of employment. An accident had taken off his right arm at the shoulder. Booze had done the rest. When Paul Pry found the man he was a human derelict, seated on the sidewalk by the corner of a bank building, holding a derby hat in his left hand. The hat was half filled with pencils, with a few small coins at the bottom.

Paul Pry had dropped in half a dollar, taken out one pencil and then been interested in something he had seen in the rugged weather-beaten face, in the flash of gratitude which had filled the unwinking glassy eyes. He had engaged him in conversation and had learned that the man was a veritable encyclopedia of underworld knowledge.

That had been the last day Mugs Magoo had known want. It marked the formation of a strange association by which Mugs furnished Paul Pry with information and the chain-lightning mind of Paul Pry translated that information to pecuniary advantage.

Mugs Magoo rolled his glassy eyes in another survey of the room and then turned once more to Paul Pry.

"Here's probably what's happening," he said. "Frank Bostwick, the lawyer is making a deal with Edgar Patten, the adjustor for the insurance company, to get Tompkins out with a light sentence or maybe get him turned loose without even a trial. The price he's going to pay is the return of the Legget diamond.

"The cops have got a dead open-and-shut case on Tompkins but they haven't been able to find the diamond. Tompkins is an old hand at the game and he's sitting tight."

"Then," said Paul Pry, "you think that Bostwick knows where the diamond is?"

Mugs Magoo stared at the table where Tom Meek was dining in solitude. "I wouldn't doubt," he said, "but what Bostwick has worked up a deal with Patten and smuggled a letter in to Tompkins by Meek. Then Tompkins has sent a reply back and Meek has got it to deliver."

"Why doesn't Meek deliver it then?" Pry wanted to know.

"That's not the way Meek works," said Mugs Magoo. "He's one of those cagey individuals that never comes out with anything in the open. He'll sit around there and eat his dinner. Then he'll get up and leave the place. The letter will be planted under his plate or under his napkin somewhere, and Bostwick will go over and get it. Then Bostwick will get in touch with Patten and they'll fix up the deal between them."

Paul Pry surveyed the dining room of the speakeasy with wary eyes that missed nothing.

"I could," said Mugs Magoo plaintively, "stand another bottle of that wine."

Paul Pry summoned the waiter. "Another pint," he said.

Mugs Magoo made a grimace. "A pint," he said, "is a half-bottle."

"A quart, waiter," Paul Pry remarked.

126

Mugs Magoo nodded his satisfaction. "Gonna telephone," he said. "Be back by the time the wine gets here."

He scraped back his chair and started in the general direction of the telephones.

It was at that moment that Tom Meek summoned the waiter, paid his check, and arose from the table. He was halfway to the door when the light dimmed to a pale blue effect of imitation moonlight and the orchestra struck up a seductive waltz.

In the confusion of the milling couples on the floor and other couples rising spontaneously from tables and twining into each other's arms, Frank Bostwick, the lawyer, got to his feet and unobtrusively started toward the table which Meek had vacated.

Paul Pry took instant advantage of the opportunity and the confusion. As swiftly and noiselessly as a trout, gliding through the black depths of a mountain pool, he slipped over to the table where Meek had been sitting. His hands made a questioning exploration of the table. The tips of the searching fingers encountered some flat object beneath the table-cloth and within a very few moments the flat object had been transferred to Paul Pry's hand.

It was a letter folded and sealed, and Paul

Pry made no attempt to read it but folded it once again and thrust it into his shoe. Then he swung slightly to one side and paused before a table where a woman was seated.

The woman was one of a trio who had entered the speakeasy, either the mother or the older sister of the young woman who accompanied her, and who was at the moment sliding into the first steps of the waltz with the young man of the party. She was amazed and flattered at Paul Pry's attention and, after a moment, when startled surprise gave way to simpering acquiescence in her expression, she permitted herself to be guided out to the center of the room which was reserved for the dance floor.

Paul Pry moved gracefully in the steps of the waltz. He had an opportunity to peer over the woman's shoulder and see that Frank Bostwick, the lawyer, was seated at the table that had been vacated by Tom Meek, the letter smuggler.

And Paul Pry's smile became a chuckle as he realized that the attorney had not observed the surreptitious theft of the missive that Tom Meek had left beneath the table-cloth.

Paul Pry was a handsome individual. More-over, he had a ready poise and a magnetic manner. His companion was grateful and pleased. And, as Paul Pry returned her to her table at the termination of the waltz, he gave to the older woman the triumph of waiting a few moments until the younger couple had returned to the table. Nor did the sharp eyes of Paul Pry miss the sudden look of incredulous surprise on the face of the younger woman, or the expression of triumphant elation upon the face of the woman with whom he had been dancing.

Then Paul Pry bowed from the waist, muttered his pleasure, and returned once more to his own table.

The chair in which Mugs Magoo had been sitting was now occupied by a woman some twenty-seven years of age. She had a wil-lowy figure, a daring backless gown, and blue eyes that stared at Paul Pry with frank invitation.

Paul Pry paused. "I beg your pardon," he said.

The woman's eyes rested upon his face with a directness of gaze that was frankly seductive. The sensuous red lips parted in a smile.

"You should," she said.

Paul Pry raised his eyebrows.

"Not," said the young woman still smiling, "that I object so much to your appearance, as to the stereotyped manner in which you have tried to pick me up. I presume you will pretend that this was your table and—" She broke off abruptly with an expression of dismay suffusing her features. "Good heavens!" she said. "It *is* your table!"

Paul Pry remained standing and smiling.

"Oh!" she said. "I'm so sorry. I had left the room and the lights went down. You see, my escort was called away on a business matter and I returned to my table alone. I just became confused, I guess."

She made a motion as if to rise, but her wide blue eyes remained fastened steadily upon Paul Pry's face.

"Well," he said, "since you're here, and since, apparently, your escort has left, why not finish the evening with me?"

"Oh, no!" she said. "I couldn't. Please don't misunderstand. I assure you it was just an accident."

"Of course it was an accident," Paul Pry said and pulled out the other chair, sat down and smiled across at her. "The sort of an accident," he went on, "that fate sometimes throws in the way of a lone man who appreciates wide blue eyes and coppery hair."

"Flatterer!" she exclaimed.

Paul Pry, glancing up at that moment, saw Mugs Magoo walking toward the table. And Mugs Magoo abruptly became conscious of the woman who was seated opposite Paul Pry.

The camera-eye man stopped dead in his tracks while his glassy eyes flickered over the features of the woman. Then Mugs Magoo raised his left hand to his ear lobe and tugged at it once, sharply. Then he turned and walked away.

In the course of the association which had grown up between the two adventurers, it had been necessary to arrange an elaborate code of signals, so that, in times of emergency, Mugs Magoo might convey complete ideas to Paul Pry by a single sign. And in their code, the gestures Mugs had just completed meant: "The party who is talking to you knows me and is dangerous. I'm getting under cover so I won't be recognized. You must extricate yourself from a dangerous position at once."

2

As a Highwayman

It was as Mugs Magoo turned away, that the cooing voice of the young woman reached Paul Pry's ears.

"Well," she said, "since you're so attractive and so nice about it, perhaps I will make an exception just this once. Won't it be a lark going through the evening pretending that we're old acquaintances, and each of us not really knowing who the other is. You may call me Stella. And your name?"

"Wonderful!" exclaimed Paul Pry with enthusiasm. "You may call me Paul."

"And we're old friends, Paul, meeting for the first time after an absence of years?"

"Yes," he said, "but don't make the absence too long. It doesn't sound plausible. Having once known you, a man would never permit too great an interval of separation."

She laughed lightly. "And so you believe in fate?" she asked.

Paul Pry nodded, his lips smiling but his eyes watchful.

"Perhaps," she said, "it was, after all,

fate." She sighed, and for the first time since she had sat at his table, lowered her eyes.

"What is fate?" asked Paul Pry.

"The fact that I should meet you just when I needed someone . . ." Her voice trailed off into silence and she shook her head vehemently.

"No," she said decisively, "I mustn't go into that."

The orchestra struck up a rollicking one-step. The blue eyes once more impacted full upon his face.

"And do we dance, Paul?" she asked.

He nodded and rose, taking the back of her chair in his hand, moving it away from the table as she swung up, in front of him, her arms open, her lips smiling invitingly.

They moved out onto the floor, a couple well calculated to catch the eye of any connoisseur of the dance. Paul Pry, moving as gracefully and lightly as though his feet had been floating on air just above the floor, the girl well curved but willowy, straight-limbed and radiating a consciousness of her sex.

"Do you know," she said, "that I was contemplating suicide earlier in the evening?"

Paul Pry tightened his arms in a gesture

of protection. "You're joking," he exclaimed.

"No," she said. "It's a fact."

"Would you care to tell me about it?" he asked.

"I think," she said slowly, "I would."

They danced for a few moments in silence and in some subtle way she managed to convey the impression that she had thrown herself entirely upon his masculine strength as a bulwark of protection. "But," she added after the interval of silence, "I couldn't tell you here."

"Where?" he asked.

"I have an apartment," she said, "if you care to come there."

"Splendid," Paul Pry said enthusiastically.

"Let's go then," she told him. "I was here only for the excitement. Only to get my mind away from myself. Now you've given me just the stimulus that I need to restore my perspective."

The music stopped.

She gave just the faintest hint of pressing her body close to his and then managed to forestall the intimacy of the moment and become, once more, respectably distant, standing with her hand on his arm, her frank blue eyes smiling into his.

"A wonderful dance," he said applauding.

"You dance divinely," she breathed.

There was no encore. She gently exerted pressure on his arm.

"Would you care to leave now?" she asked.

"Yes, indeed," he told her.

Paul Pry lived by his wits and he was an opportunist. Moreover, he was, as Mugs Magoo so frequently pointed out, entirely without prudence. Paul Pry would walk into any danger which offered a reasonable amount of excitement, and do it with the utmost *sangfroid*, trusting to his ingenuity to extricate himself from any untoward complications.

Paul Pry, upon this occasion, took only a reasonable amount of precaution to ascertain that he was not being shadowed as he left the cabaret. Having satisfied himself that no one was on his trail, he handed the young woman into a taxicab, followed her, and was lighting a cigarette as the cab driver slammed the door and nodded his comprehension of the address the young woman had given him.

It was but a short ride to the apartment and Paul Pry followed docilely into the elevator, out of the car again, and down a corridor. A close observer would have noticed that his right hand hovered near the left lapel of his coat as the young woman opened the door of the apartment and switched on the lights. But a moment later his hand was back at his side, for the apartment was, quite apparently, empty, unless someone were concealed behind a closed door. And Paul Pry always claimed that he could get a gun from its holster long before a person could twist the knob of a door, open it and draw a bead.

"My God, Paul," she said, "I'm glad that I met you!"

Paul Pry watched the outer door of the apartment move slowly shut until the spring lock automatically clicked into position and then smiled at her. "It was," he said, "a real pleasure to me, Stella."

"And," she said, smiling at him with half-parted lips and steady eyes, "we're old friends. Wasn't that the understanding, Paul?"

"Yes, Stella."

"Very well then," she said, "I'm going to get out of these clothes and get into something comfortable. Wait here and make yourself at home."

Paul Pry's hand once more hovered about the lapel of his coat as she opened the door of the connecting bedroom, but the door closed without event and Paul Pry moved to a chair which gave him a commanding position, sat down, crossed his knees and lit a cigarette.

Five minutes later the bedroom door opened and Stella came out, a vision of filmy loveliness. And it may or may not have been accident that she had placed a very bright light directly behind her, that she stood for a long moment in the doorway of the bedroom before switching out the light, and that the brilliant illumination transformed her silken coverings into a mere filmy aura which served to frame, without concealing, her every curve.

She switched out the light and came to him.

She perched on the arm of his chair; her fingers smoothed his hair; one leg swinging free in a pendulum-like arc, swung clear of the filmy silken covering.

"Paul," she said, "really and truly I feel as though I've known you all my life."

"Go ahead then," he said, "and confide in me."

She sighed and her hands dropped from his hair, brushed lightly along his cheek and then came to rest on his shoulders.

"Paul," she said, "don't look at me while I tell you. I can't bear that. Sit just as you are and listen."

"Listening," he told her.

"Did you ever hear of a man called 'Silver' Dawson?"

"No," said Paul Pry. "Who is Silver Dawson?"

"The worst fiend unhung," she said with vehemence.

"That still leaves a lot to my imagination," Paul Pry reminded.

"He's got the letters," she told him.

"What letters?"

"The letters that I wrote to a man who betrayed my confidence."

"Indeed?" said Paul Pry.

"Yes," she said. "And you see I was married at the time."

"Ah," said Paul Pry in a tone of quickening interest, "and you're married now?"

"No, my husband is dead."

"I see," he said, in a tone of one who waits for further revelations.

"But he left this peculiar will," she said, "in which my inheritance was predicated upon my fidelity. The will contained a proviso that if it should appear I had been unfaithful to him during our married life, the inheritance was to go to a charitable institution."

"I see," said Paul Pry, "and the letters threaten to complicate things?"

"The letters," she said, "would ruin me."

"You shouldn't have written them," he told her.

She slid her palm under his chin, tilted his head so that her eyes could stare down into his. "Tell me," she said, "did you ever do anything that you shouldn't have done?"

"Lots of times," he said.

"All right then. So have I."

Paul Pry laughed and patted her hand.

"And," she said meaningfully, "I intend to do other things that I shouldn't do. It's lots of fun. But I don't like to lose an inheritance on account of an innocent affair."

"Innocent?" he asked.

"Yes," she said. "Of course."

"Then the letters can't be so very bad," he told her.

"The letters," she said archly, "are quite likely to be misunderstood. You understand I have always been a woman of restrictions and inhibitions. It goes back to the time of my girlhood. I was brought up by old-fashioned parents and I was the victim of a too puritanical training. As a result, when I started to write, all of my repressed desires came to the front and were manifest in the letters."

"I take it, then," said Paul Pry, "the letters would not listen well in front of a jury."

"Well," she said judicially, "unless the members of the jury were pretty well up on love-making they'd get some great ideas."

"Therefore," said Paul Pry, "you do not wish to have the letters read before a jury."

"Naturally."

"What," asked Paul Pry, "does Silver Dawson say about it?"

"He's a cold-blooded snake," she said. "He's called Silver because of his shock of white hair, that makes him look old, patient, dignified and sort of grand. But he'd steal the pennies off the eyes of a corpse."

"Naturally," said Paul Pry, "he has some proposition to offer."

"Yes," she said. "It's ruinous."

"Certainly," said Paul Pry, "he wouldn't want more than a percentage of what you inherited."

"It isn't money he wants," she said. "He wants things that I cannot give."

Her voice lowered until it was hardly more than a whisper.

"He said that I must go to Europe with him."

Her face took on an expression of virginal, injured innocence. Her eyes seemed limpid with tears that were about to spring to the surface and she stared pathetically at Paul Pry.

"And what do you intend to do?" asked Paul Pry.

"I told you," she said, "I was going to commit suicide."

"Now you've changed your mind?" he asked her, petting her hand.

"Yes. I've so much to live for—now."

"Well," pressed Paul Pry, "haven't you any scheme?"

She looked at him in impersonal appraisal. Just the sort of a glance which a scientist might give to an impaled butterfly before classifying it.

"Well," she said slowly, "I have a scheme which I was thinking of while we were dancing. You seemed so graceful and well knit, so poised and completely able to take care of yourself, that a wild idea flashed through my head. But I'm afraid that it's hardly practicable, and it's something I have no right to ask a virtual stranger."

"An old friend, Stella," he said, patting her hand.

"Very well then," she said, "as an old friend you're entitled to hear the scheme, and—to have the prerogatives of an old friendship."

She leaned forward and kissed him lingeringly, full upon the lips.

"Ah," said Paul Pry. "The duties of such a friendship certainly cannot detract from its net advantage!"

She laughed and pinched his cheek. "Silly boy!" she said.

Paul Pry said nothing, but sat waiting.

Once more the blue eyes gave him that appraising glance, and then she spoke in low, throaty tones.

"Silver Dawson has a certain circle of acquaintances, not in the best class of society but, nevertheless, a wealthy class. He's giving a masquerade party tomorrow night

142

at his house. I just had an idea that you might capitalize on that. You see, the guests will be in all sorts of costumes. I thought it might be possible for you to go as a highwayman."

"A highwayman?" asked Paul Pry.

"Yes. You know with a mask and a gun and everything. It would make an interesting costume."

"But," said Paul Pry, "what good would it do?"

"Simply this," she said. "You could break away from the dance and move around the house. I could show you where the papers were. If you encountered any of the servants or anyone, you could pull your gun and act the part of a highwayman. If anything went wrong you could claim that it was merely in fun as a part of the masquerade.

"But nothing will go wrong. You can get in and get the papers. I know exactly where he keeps them. Then you could mingle with the guests, attract attention for your unusual costume, slip out and join me on the outside."

"But," said Paul Pry, "I have no invitation."

"You wouldn't need any," she said.

"There is a ladder in the back of the house and we could put it up to one of the second-story windows. Those are always unlocked. You could climb in."

"No," said Paul Pry slowly, "that wouldn't be such a good scheme. It would be better to try and crash the party. I might forge an invitation."

"There's a thought!" she exclaimed. "I could get you an invitation. You could walk right in the front door and then you could slip away from the crowd and go up to his study where he keeps the letters."

"But they would be under lock and key, wouldn't they?"

"No. That is, they'd be in a desk and the desk has a lock on it; but you could handle that lock easily enough. I think I could get you a skeleton key that would work it."

Paul Pry slipped an arm about her waist. "I'll do it, Stella," he said, "for an old friend."

She laughed throatily. "Such a gallant creature," she said, "deserves another— prerogative of friendship."

She leaned forward.

Murder Masquerade

Mugs Magoo was seated in the apartment when Paul Pry latchkeyed the door and walked in. Magoo looked up in glassy-eyed appraisal. Then he reached for the half-filled whiskey bottle at this elbow, poured out a generous drink in a tumbler and drained it with a single motion.

"Well," he said, "I never expected to see you again."

"You always were a cheerful cuss," said Paul Pry, depositing his coat and hat in the closet.

"Just a fool for luck," said Mugs Magoo jovially. "You've had an appointment that's six months overdue that I know of. There's a marble slab all picked out for you and why you haven't been on it for a long time is more than I know."

"Mugs," said Paul Pry laughing, "you're a natural pessimist."

"Pessimist nothing," said Mugs. "You disregard signals, you walk into the damndest traps and how you ever get out is more than I know."

"How do you mean?" asked Paul Pry.

"The woman that was with you at the table," Mugs Magoo said, "was 'Slick' Stella Molay, and she was covering Tom Meek. I saw you slip over and get the letter and she saw you, too. Frank Bostwick is just a lawyer. He's all right to stand up in front of a jury and wave his arms and talk about the Constitution, but he isn't fast on his feet. That's why Tompkins had Slick Stella Molay follow Tom Meek to make sure that the letter got delivered."

"I see," said Paul Pry. "Then Slick Stella knew that I had the letter. Is that it?"

"Of course she did."

"Why didn't she accuse me of it, or try to steal it?"

"Because she knew it wouldn't do any good. She knew that you were wise to the play and that you were going to read the letter."

"What did she want with me then?" asked Paul Pry.

Mugs Magoo gave a snorting gesture of disgust. "Want with you!" he exclaimed. "She wanted to get you out of the way, of course. She wanted to put you where you'll be pushing up daisies."

Paul Pry grinned gleefully. "Well," he said, "I'm still here."

"Still here because of that providence which watches over fools and idiots," Mugs Magoo told him. "With the chances you take and the way you walk into trouble, it's a wonder you haven't been killed months ago. Why, do you know that Slick Stella Molay is the one who got 'Big' Ben Desmond killed in Chicago?"

"Indeed," said Paul Pry, raising polite eyebrows, "and how did Big Ben Desmond cash in? Did she shoot him or use poison?"

Mugs Magoo poured himself another drink of whiskey. "Not that baby," he said. "She's too slick for that."

"All right," said Paul Pry, "I confess to my interest, Mugs. Go ahead and quit keeping me in suspense."

"Well," said Mugs Magoo, "it was so slick there wasn't a flaw in it. The grand jury looked it all over and couldn't do anything about it."

Paul Pry relaxed comfortably in a reclining chair, lit a cigarette and let his face show polite interest.

"Do you mean to say, Mugs, that a person could murder another, under such circumstances that a grand jury could look it over and couldn't find anything wrong with it?"

"Slick Stella Molay could," said Mugs Magoo.

"And just how did she do it?"

"She got Big Ben Desmond sold on the idea that he was to go to a masquerade ball dressed as a highwayman. Then she got him to go prowling around the house of the man that was giving the masquerade. That man was in his bedroom standing in front of a wall safe, putting some jewelry away, when he heard the sound of a door opening. He turned around and saw a man dressed like a crook, with gloves and a mask, a gun and all the rest of it.

"The guy who was giving the party was heeled, and he just snapped up his gun and plopped five shells into Big Ben Dawson's guts before he found out that he was shooting a guest who had just been walking around the house in a masquerade costume."

Paul Pry yawned and stifled the yawn with four polite fingers.

"Indeed, Mugs," he said. "Rather crude.

148

I had thought it might be sufficiently novel to be interesting."

"Well," said Mugs Magoo, "it was novel enough to get Big Ben Desmond out of the way; and the grand jury couldn't do anything to the guy that killed him because they claimed the guy was entitled to shoot a burglar. And Slick Stella Molay was out in the clear. She put an onion in her handkerchief, went before the grand jury full of weeps and red-eyed grief. They say her eyes looked like hell when she was testifying, but she was damned careful her legs were all right. She wore the best pair of stockings in her wardrobe and when she crossed her knees the grand jury decided that, no matter what had happened, Slick Stella didn't know anything about it."

"And so," asked Paul Pry, "you think she'd like to get me out of the way?"

"Sure she would. What was in the letter?"

"I don't know."

Mugs Magoo sat bolt upright in his chair and stared with protruding, glassy eyes at Paul Pry.

"You mean to say that you don't know what's in the letter?"

"No. I haven't the faintest idea."

"Well, what the devil did you take the letter for?"

"To read, of course."

"Well, why didn't you read it?"

"I put it down in my shoe and haven't had a chance," said Paul Pry.

Casually, as if the matter were of minor importance, he took the envelope from his shoe, opened his penknife with great deliberation, and slit the envelope along the side. He shook out a folded piece of paper.

"What's it say?" asked Mugs Magoo eagerly.

Paul Pry frowned.

"Rather a puzzling message, I should say, Mugs."

"Well, what is it?"

Paul Pry read the letter out loud—"Tell Stella there's a screw loose, it's Bunny's nutcracker and to make the play but spring me before you flash the take."

"Is that all of it?" asked Mugs Magoo.

"That's all of it," said Paul Pry.

"Well," said Mugs, "we know now why Stella was sticking around that lawyer. Frank Bostwick would never have known what that meant."

"Do you know?" asked Paul Pry.

150

"Well," said Mugs Magoo, regarding the diminishing level of amber fluid in the whiskey bottle with a mournful expression, "there's some things about it I don't understand. Bunny must be Bunny Myers and when Tompkins says to spring him before flashing the take, it means that he's to actually be out of jail before they exhibit the diamond or turn it over to the insurance company."

"Do you suppose that means that there's something phony about the diamond?" asked Paul Pry.

Mugs said: "Tompkins wouldn't dare to deliver a phony gem to the insurance company. But he's just playing cautious. Lots of times the insurance companies make promises about what they'll do with the district attorney if the crook will come through and tell the hiding place of the gem. Then, when it comes to a showdown, and the insurance company is in the clear, they lose all interest in the matter and the crook gets about twice as stiff a jolt as he would otherwise have drawn."

"Tell me some more about Bunny Myers," said Paul Pry.

"He's an undersized guy with mild eyes

and a big nose and rabbit teeth. They stick out in front and make you feel like feeding him a carrot whenever you see him. I haven't run across Bunny for four or five years; but I know that he used to run around with Tompkins on some of the gem stuff.

"Bunny is a good man to have along because he's so harmless. He looks like a regular rabbit and damned if he don't act like one."

"Any great amount of ability?" asked Paul Pry.

"Yes, he's pretty fast with his noodle," Mugs Magoo admitted, "and he's a pretty good actor. He's cultivated that manner of meekness because nobody ever expects a stick-up artist to have such a meek appearance."

"Well," said Paul Pry, "there's no use bothering my head about it. The message is in some sort of code and it doesn't seem to help us very much. I've got to get my beauty sleep, because I've got a hard night ahead of me tomorrow night."

"Pulling a job tomorrow night?" asked Mugs Magoo, showing interest.

"No," said Paul Pry, "I'm going out to a ball tomorrow night."

"What sort of a ball?" Mugs Magoo inquired.

"A ball that Slick Stella Molay wants me to go to with her," said Paul Pry. "She's going to arrange for an invitation. I'm going in rather a unique costume. She's worked it all out for me, Mugs. It's rather novel. I'm going as a conventional burglar, dressed in a mask and carrying a gun and kit of burglar tools."

Mugs Magoo whirled around and the whiskey bottle, struck by his shoulder, toppled for a moment and crashed to the floor.

"You're what?" he yelled.

"Don't shout," said Paul Pry. "I'm merely going to a masquerade ball with Slick Stella Molay, dressed as a burglar."

Mugs Magoo shook his head dolefully. His hand went to his forehead, as though trying to hold his brain to some semblance of sanity by physical pressure.

"Oh, my God!" he groaned.

"And, by the way," said Paul Pry, "undoubtedly, you're correct in your assumption that Stella knows I picked up the letter Tom Meek left for the lawyer. They'll try to get another one smuggled out of the jail. How long will it take them?"

Mugs Magoo shook his head lugubriously from side to side.

"As far as that's concerned," he said, "it'll probably take them a couple of days. They've got to smuggle a message in to Tompkins and then Tompkins has got to get another letter to Meek and have it delivered. But you don't need to worry about it, guy. You won't be here when it happens. You'll be lying flat on your back with a lily in your hand. You were a good pal while you lasted but you're like the pitcher that went to the well too often.

"I don't want to intrude on your private affairs, but if you'd let me know the songs that you like best, I'll see that the undertaker gives you the breaks when it comes to the music."

4

Bunny's Nutcracker

The cab driver swung in behind the line of cars that crawled along close to the curb and Slick Stella Molay said: "This is the place."

Within a few seconds Paul Pry was handing Stella out from the taxicab and receiving her gracious smile.

"Darling," she said, "you look splendid. You make my heart go pitty-pat. You look exactly like a burglar."

Paul Pry accepted the compliment and paid off the taxi driver.

"I'll say he looks like a burglar," said the taxi driver, pocketing the money. "It was all I could do to keep from shelling out instead of handing him the meter slip. You see, lady, I was stuck up a week ago and my stomach still feels cold where the gun was pointed."

"And, so this," said Paul Pry, "is the lair of the famous Silver Dawson?"

"Yes," she said. "He's the blackmail king of the underworld. He's a fighter. I wish someone would kill him."

"Will I meet him," asked Paul Pry, "as we go in?"

"No," she said. "Simply show your invitation to the man at the door and then we'll go in and mingle with the crowd for a minute, have a drink of punch and perhaps a dance. After that you go upstairs. The study is the room on the front of the house on the second floor and the papers are there in the desk. I've given you the key."

"Then what?" asked Paul Pry.

"Then," she said, "we mingle around with the crowd a little longer and then go back to the apartment."

"Without unmasking?" asked Paul Pry.

"Without unmasking," she said. "I would have to unmask if you did, and if Silver Dawson saw me here he'd know right away something was wrong and that our invitations had been forged."

"And if I should meet any of the servants?" asked Paul Pry.

"Then," she said, "go ahead and stick a gun in their ribs. Tie them and gag them if you have to, or knock them out. You don't need to worry, because if anybody should touch you, you could claim that you were looking for the restroom."

She turned and flashed him a dazzling

look from her wide blue eyes, a smile from her sensuous, parted lips.

"You see," she said, "everybody would know that you had attended the masquerade in this costume so it would be all right."

Paul Pry nodded. "All right," he said, "let's go."

They walked into the house, surrendered their forged invitations to a doorman and mingled with the crowd. A dozen or more couples were already hilarious from the effects of a remarkably strong punch which was being dished out in quantities by an urbane individual in evening clothes, who had a napkin hanging over his left forearm.

Paul Pry escorted Stella to the punch bowl and, after the second drink of punch, she whirled him out to the floor as the orchestra struck up a dance.

She held herself close to him and whispered words of soft endearment in his ear as they moved lightly across the floor.

"Darling," she said, "you'd be surprised at how grateful I'm going to be."

"Yes?" he asked.

"Yes," she said. "The prerogatives of a long friendship, you know."

Paul Pry missed a step and suddenly tightened his arms about the willowy figure in order to let her understand his appreciation.

"I think," she cooed, leaning toward him so that her lips were close to his, "we had better swing over toward this darkest corner by the door. That door leads to the hallway and you go up the stairs and into the front room. I think Silver Dawson is the man dressed in the red devil suit over there by the punch bowl. I'm quite certain there won't be anyone on the upper floor. I've kept my eyes open, getting the servants spotted, and I'm sure they're all downstairs."

"You seem to know the house quite well," said Paul Pry.

"Yes," she said, "I have been here several times before. Sometimes as a guest and more recently as a suppliant, offering anything to get the letters back."

"Anything?" asked Paul Pry.

"Almost anything," she said softly.

The music stopped. Stella pressed her form close to Paul Pry's for one tantalizing moment, then breathed softly: "Hurry, dear, and then we can leave."

Paul Pry nodded and slipped unostentatiously through the doorway into the dark hall.

There were no servants in sight. A flight of stairs led to the upper corridor and Paul Pry took them on swiftly silent feet, moving with a light grace and catlike speed.

But Paul Pry did not turn to the left and go toward the front of the house. Instead he flattened himself against a door which opened upon the corridor near the head of the stairs, and listened carefully.

After a second or two he dropped to his hands and knees and tried the knob of the door.

The door swung inward and Paul Pry, lying prone on the floor, where he would be clear of the line of fire in the event anyone should have been standing in the doorway, peered into the dark interior of the room.

There was no sound or motion. The room was a bedroom and the light which filtered in from the hallway showed a walnut bed, a dressing table and bureau.

There was a ribbon of light which seeped through from the bottom of a door at the other end of the room.

Paul Pry got to his feet, moved swiftly and silently, stepped into the room and closed the door behind him. Then he walked purposefully toward the door where he could see the ribbon of light.

He was more confident as he tried the knob of this door, but equally careful to make no sound. He leaned his weight against the door so as to remove any tension from the latch, turned the knob very slowly to eliminate any possibility of noise. When the catch was free, he pulled the door toward him a bit at a time.

The door opened and Paul Pry, peering through, saw that he was looking into a bathroom, sumptuously appointed. At the other side of the bathroom was a door paneled with a full-length mirror.

Paul Pry stepped into the bathroom and turned out the light by the simple expedient of unscrewing the globe a half turn. Then he devoted his attention to the knob of the opposite doorway.

That knob slowly turned till the catch was free and Paul Pry opened the door an inch at a time.

The bathroom was now dark, so that there was no light behind him to pour into the room as the door was opened.

This door opened into the study which Stella had pointed out to him as being at the front of the house, and the place where the desk was located that contained the precious letters.

A floor lamp was arranged with the shade tilted so that the rays of light were directed full against a door, which Paul Pry surmised must be the door into the corridor and through which he had been supposed to make his entrance.

Standing in the shadows, back of that light, his eyes cold and grim, a heavy automatic held in his right hand, was an undersized man with a sloping forehead, a large nose and rabbit teeth that showed through his half-parted lips.

Noiselessly Paul Pry swung the door open and stepped into the room upon catlike feet.

He had made three steps before some slight noise or perhaps some intuition warned the man with the gun. He whirled with an exclamation of surprise and raised the weapon.

Paul Pry swung swiftly with his right fist. At the same time he leaped forward.

There was the sound of the hissing exclamation of surprise which came from the man with the gun, the noise of swiftly shuffling feet, the impact of a fist on flesh and then a half groan as the man with the rabbit teeth sank to the carpeted floor.

Paul Pry pocketed the gun. "Make a sound," he said, "and I'll slit your throat."

But the man on the floor was limp and unconscious.

Paul Pry moved swiftly. A handkerchief was thrust into the man's mouth, a bit of strong cord from his pocket looped around the man's wrist and bit into the flesh. Then Paul Pry's hands darted swiftly and purposefully through the man's clothing.

He found a roll of bills, a penknife, cigarette lighter, cigarette case, a handkerchief, fountain pen, some small change, a leather key container well filled with keys, and a blackjack.

The blackjack, hung from a light cord under the left armpit, was worn and shiny from much carrying. It had a conventional leather thong looped around the handle so that it could circle a man's writs in time of necessity.

Paul Pry jerked the slungshot free and put it in his pocket. He also pocketed the roll of currency. Then he arose, took the keys and moved swiftly about the room, opening locked drawers and the cover of a roll-top desk.

It was at the back of a drawer of the desk that Paul Pry found a packet of letters tied with ribbon. He unfastened the ribbon and glanced swiftly at some of the letters.

The cursory examination showed that they were letters in a feminine handwriting, addressed to "Dearest Bunny" and signed "your own, Stella" in some instances, and "your darling red-hot mamma, Stella" in others.

Paul Pry slipped the letters into his pocket, gave a last swift glance at the figure on the floor and stepped into the bathroom. He walked across the bathroom, through the darkened bedroom, out into the corridor and down the stairs.

Stella Molay was standing in the hallway at the foot of the stairs. Her head was cocked slightly to one side, after the manner of one who is listening, momentarily expecting some noise to crash out on the stillness of the night. A noise which can well be followed by a feminine scream.

As Paul Pry crept lithely down the stairs she stared at him with wide incredulous eyes.

"Good God!" she said. "What's happened!"

Paul Pry walked across to her and made

a low bow. "Congratulations, dear," he said. "Your honor is safe."

He straightened to stare into the incredulous dismay of the wide blue eyes.

"Where's Bunny?" she asked.

"Bunny?" he said.

"I mean Silver. Silver Dawson," she corrected herself hastily. "A short man with funny teeth and a big nose."

"Oh," said Paul Pry, "he's in the ballroom. Don't you remember? The man in the devil suit standing over by the punch bowl."

She looked at him with a sudden glint of suspicion in the blue eyes, but Paul Pry returned her stare with a look of childlike candor.

"Well," he said, "let's get out of here and go to the apartment."

"Look here," she said suspiciously, "there's something wrong. You must have got the wrong letters."

"What makes you think so?"

She bit her lip and then said slowly: "Just a hunch, that's all."

Paul Pry gently took her arm. "I'm quite sure it's all right," he said. "I've got the letters."

She paused for a moment as though trying

to think up some excuse and then reluctantly accompanied him through the door, across the porch, and down to the line of cars where Paul Pry summoned a cab that was waiting on the off chance of picking up a bit of business.

Once within the taxicab, Paul Pry switched on the dome light and took the letters from his pocket.

"You must be sure you've got the right letters," she said. "Otherwise, you'll have to go back. The letters that I wrote were—quite indiscreet."

"Well," said Paul Pry, pulling one of the letters from the envelope, "let's see if this is indiscreet enough."

He unfolded the letter while she leaned toward him to stare over his shoulder.

As her eyes saw the writing, she gave a gasp. "The damn fool," she said, "to have saved those!"

Paul Pry, apparently heedless of the remark, read a line aloud and then broke into a chuckle. "Certainly," he said, "that's indiscreet enough for you."

She snatched the letter from his hand, stared at him with blazing eyes.

"Come, sweetheart," he said, "and give

me another of those prerogatives of friendship."

Mugs Magoo stood up as Paul Pry entered
the room and gave a dramatic imitation of
one who is seeing a ghost.

He swung his arm across his eyes.

"Go away!" he shouted. "Go away! Don't
hurt me! I was good to him in his lifetime!
His ghost can't haunt me! Get away, I say!"

Paul Pry dropped into a chair without
bothering to remove either his topcoat or
his hat. He lit a cigarette and thrust it in
his smiling lips at a jaunty angle.

"What's the matter, Mugs?" he asked.

"My God," said Mugs, "it talks! A ghost
that talks! I know it can't be you, because
you're dead! You were killed tonight, but
how is it that your ghost doesn't have any
bullet holes in its body? And it's the first
time in my life I ever saw a ghost smoke a
cigarette!"

Paul Pry laughed and his hand, dropping
to his trouser pocket, brought out a roll of
bills. Carelessly, he tossed them to the table.

Mugs stared at the roll. "How much?"
he asked.

"Oh, five or six thousand," said Paul Pry
carelessly.

"What!" Mugs exclaimed.

Paul Pry nodded.

"Where did it come from?"

"Well," said Paul Pry, "part of it was a donation that was made to me by Bunny Myers. It was an involuntary donation and Bunny will probably not recall it when he wakes up, but it was a donation, nevertheless."

"And the rest?" asked Mugs Magoo.

Paul Pry settled himself more comfortably in his chair.

"Do you know, Mugs," he said, "I got the idea that possibly Tompkins didn't trust even his own gang. He had concealed the gem where no one knew where it was. That was a funny crack he made in the note about Bunny's nutcracker. So when Bunny Myers was making his involuntary donation to me, I examined the slungshot that he carried under his arm.

"Sure enough, there was a screw loose in it. Rather the whole handle could be unscrewed, by exerting proper pressure. Evidently, it was a slungshot that Tompkins had given to Bunny and one he intended to use in a pinch as a receptacle for something that was too hot for him to handle.

"When I unscrewed it, I found the Legget diamond, and a very affable gentleman by the name of Mr. Edgar Patten, an adjuster for the insurance company that handled the insurance on the gem, was good enough to insist that I take a slight reward for my services when I returned the stone to him."

Mugs Magoo pursed his lips and gave a low whistle. "Just a fool for luck!" he exclaimed. "You sure picked two of the toughest nuts in the game, and you're still alive! It ain't right!"

Paul Pry chuckled softly. "Tough nuts to crack all right, Mugs," he mused, "but, with the aid of Bunny's nutcracker, I managed all right."

The Cross-Stitch Killer

Millionaires were that hunter's only game, and when he'd bagged them he sewed their lips up tight for he knew that even dead men sometimes talk. But Paul Pry, professional opportunist, was a tailor of sorts himself, with a needle as sharp and deadly as the cross-stitch killer's— an avenging sword cane to darn living flesh!

─1─

Murdered Millions

Paul Pry polished the razor-keen blade of his sword cane with the same attentive care a stone polisher might take in putting just the right lustre upon a fine piece of onyx.

"Mugs" Magoo sat slumped in a big over-stuffed chair in the corner. He held a whiskey glass in his left hand. His right arm was off at the shoulder.

Eva Bentley sat in a small, glass-enclosed booth and listened to a radio which was tuned in on the wave length of the police broadcasting station. From time to time she took swift notes in competent shorthand, occasionally rattled out a few paragraphs on a portable typewriter which was on a desk at her elbow.

Mugs Magoo rolled his glassy eyes in the direction of Paul Pry. "Some day," he said, "some crook is going to grab the blade of that sword cane and bust it in two. Why don't you pack a big gun and forget that sword cane business? The blade ain't big

171

enough to cut off a plug of chewing to-bacco."

Paul Pry smiled. "The efficacy of this sword cane, Mugs, lies in its lightness and speed. It's like a clever boxer who flashes in, lands a telling blow, and jumps out again before a heavier adversary can even get set to deliver a punch."

Mugs Magoo nodded his head slowly and lugubriously. "Now," he said, "I know why you like that weapon—that's the way you like to play game, jumping in ahead of the police, side-stepping the crooks, ducking out before anyone knows what's happened, and leaving a hell of a mess behind."

Paul Pry's smile broadened into a grin, and the grin became a chuckle. "Well, Mugs," he said, "there's just a chance there may be something in that."

At that moment, Eva Bentley jumped to her feet, picked up her shorthand notebook and opened the door of the glass-enclosed compartment. Instantly, the sound of the police radio became audible.

"What is it, Eva?" asked Paul Pry. "Something important?"

"Yes," she said, "there's just been an-other corpse found, with his lips sewed to-gether. Like the other one, he's a millionaire—Charles B. Darwin is the victim this time. His murder is almost identical with that of the murder of Harry Travers. Both men were stabbed to death; both men had been receiving threatening letters through the mail; both men were found dead, with their lips sewed together with a peculiar cross-stitch."

Mugs Magoo poured himself a glass of whiskey. "Thank God I ain't no millionaire!" he said.

Paul Pry finished polishing the blade of the sword cane, and inserted it in the cunningly disguised scabbard. His eyes were level-lidded in concentration, and his voice was quick and sharp.

"I presume the police are making quite a commotion about it," he said.

"I'll say they are," Eva Bentley told him. "They've broadcast a general alarm telling all cars to drop everything and concentrate on finding this mysterious murderer. It seems to be a question of money. In fact, the police are certain of it. Evidently they have some information which has not been given to the press. However, it's common knowledge that both men received letters demanding that they place a certain sum of money in an envelope and mail it to a certain person at a certain address. Both men disregarded the request and turned the letter over to the police."

"Any information about any other men who have received similar letters?" asked Paul Pry.

"None. The police are simply giving instructions to the cars. They're assigning cars to the district in which the body was found."

"Where was it—in a house."

"No, it was found in an automobile. The man had evidently been driving an automobile and had pulled in to the curb and stopped. He was killed seated at the wheel. The officers place the death as having taken place at about three o'clock this morning. They are inclined to believe there was some woman companion in the automobile with him, and they're trying to find her. They think that she knows something of the crime, or can at least give some clue to the murderer.

"Anything else?" asked Paul Pry.

"That's about all of it," she said. "You don't want the detailed instructions which are being given the automobiles, do you?"

"No," he told her, "not now. But make

notes of everything that goes over the radio in connection with this crime."

She returned to the booth, where she closed the door and once more started her pencil flying over the pages of the shorthand notebook.

Paul Pry turned to Mugs Magoo. His face was fixed in an expression of keen concentration. "All right, Mugs," he said, "snap out of it and tell me what you know about the millionaires."

Mugs Magoo groaned. "Ain't it enough for me to know about the crooks?" he asked, "without having to spill all the dope on the millionaires?"

Paul Pry laughed. "I know what you're trying to do, Mugs," he said. "You're trying to keep me from taking an interest in this case because you're afraid of it. But I'm going to take an interest in it just the same."

Mugs Magoo tilted the bottle of whiskey over the tumbler, drained the last drop from the tumbler, smacked his lips, then turned his glassy eyes toward Paul Pry.

Those were remarkable eyes. They protruded slightly and seemed dead and expressionless, as though covered with some thin, white film. But they were eyes that saw much and forgot nothing.

Mugs Magoo could give the name, antecedents, connection and criminal record of almost every known crook in the United States. Moreover, he had but to look at a face once in order to remember that man indefinitely. All gossip, all information which ever reached his ears; all occurrences which took place within the range of his vision, remained indelibly impressed upon his memory.

At one time he had been camera-eye man for the metropolitan police. A political shake-up had thrown him out of work, and an unfortunate accident had taken off his right arm at the shoulder. Feeling that he could never return to the police force he had indulged his desire for liquor, until, when Paul Pry found the man, he had been but a sodden wreck, begging a mere pittance as a cripple, by selling pencils on a street corner. Paul Pry had cultivated the man, gradually learned something of his history and the remarkable gift which had made him so valuable to the police. He had given him food, clothes, money, and an allowance of whiskey, which served to satisfy the keen craving of the man's insatiable appetite.

From time to time, he used such information as Mugs Magoo could impart by drawing upon his encyclopedic knowledge of the underworld.

"Mugs," said Paul Pry, "what do you know about Charles Darwin?"

Mugs Magoo shook his head. "Keep out of it, chief," he said. "Please keep out of it. You're mixing with dynamite. This isn't the sort of a case where you're up against some cheap crook; you're dealing with a homicidal maniac here."

Paul Pry waited for a moment, then said again with slow emphasis: "Mugs, what do you know about Charles Darwin?"

Mugs Magoo sighed. "To begin with, he's a millionaire who made his money out of the stock market when the stock market was going up, and didn't lose his money when the stock market went down. That means that he's got brains or is lucky."

"He married one of those cold-blooded society-type women, and the marriage didn't take. He got to playing around. Mrs. Darwin never played in her life; she didn't know what play was. Life was a serious proposition with her, a question of just who she should invite to the next tea, and what sort of a bid she should make when she picked up her bridge hand.

"Darwin wanted a divorce. She wouldn't give him one. She hired detectives to trail him around, so that she could get enough on him so that he couldn't get one. He could never get anything on her, because there was never anything to get."

"How do you know all this, Mugs?" asked Paul Pry curiously.

Mugs Magoo regarded the empty whiskey glass with a speculative eye. "Those glasses," he said, "don't hold as much as the others; they—"

"Never mind the glasses, Mugs. How did you find out all this about a millionaire's matrimonial mix-up?"

"Oh," said Mugs wearily, "the detective that Mrs. Darwin got hold of was an ex-con. I spotted him, and he was afraid I was going to turn him in, so he spilled the beans to me about what he was doing."

"Well," said Paul Pry, "you're still not telling me what happened."

"Well," Mugs Magoo said, "he was a clever bird. He wasn't like the ordinary private detective. Naturally he wasn't, because he'd been a high-class crook in his time, and he knew a lot of angles that only a crook would know. As a result, he got quite a bit of stuff on Darwin. He found out where Darwin was keeping a love nest."

"A love nest?" asked Paul Pry.

"Well, that's what the tabloids call it," Mugs Magoo said. "It was just an apartment he kept without letting his wife know about it."

"But his wife found out about it?" asked Pry.

"Not this one," Mugs said. "The detective found out about it, but he was too wise to report the information to the agency. He realized that all he'd draw from the agency would be eight dollars a day, perhaps a bonus of a suit of clothes, or something. So he went to Darwin, put the cards on the table, told Darwin what he had, and offered to sell out for five thousand dollars. Naturally, he got the five grand."

"And what did he tell the agency?" asked Paul Pry.

"Oh, he told the agency enough to let them make a pretty good report to Mrs. Darwin. As a matter of fact, I think he fixed it up with Charles Darwin so that the report was sufficiently complete to give Mrs. Darwin most of the evidence she wanted."

Paul Pry squinted his forehead thoughtfully. "Where was this love nest, Mugs?" he asked.

Mugs was pouring whiskey into the glass. Abruptly, he stopped and straightened. His eyes blinked thoughtfully. "Hell!" he said. "I've got the address of the place somewhere in my mind, but—by gosh!—it was out in the west end somewhere. Ain't that a break?"

Paul Pry reached for his hat and coat. "All right, Mugs," he said, "pull the address out of the back of your mind, because I want it."

———2———

Paul Pry Turns Peeping Tom

The apartment house had that subtle air of quiet exclusiveness which is associated with high prices, but not necessarily with respectability.

Paul Pry moved down the deeply carpeted corridor like some silent shadow. He paused in front of the door and inspected the lock. Then he selected a key from a well-filled key ring, inserted the key and exerted a slow, steady pressure. A moment later there was a click as the lock slipped back.

Paul Pry moved on through the door, into the apartment, and closed the door behind him.

He had, he observed with satisfaction, reached the place ahead of the police. Doubtless, the police would, sooner or later, find out about this expensive apartment which was maintained by the millionaire play-boy who had figured so grimly in such a blood-curdling murder. Right at present, however, Paul Pry was on the job, and in the position of one who is one jump ahead.

Paul Pry did not switch on the lights, but used an electric flashlight. He sent the beam darting about the apartment. He saw that the windows were covered by expensive drapes; that, in addition to the drapes, there were shades which were drawn down, making it virtually impossible for the faintest flicker of light to be seen from the street. There were expensive carpets, deep over-stuffed chairs, a well-filled bookcase which seemed, however, more to furnish background than a source of reading material. There was a bedroom with a beautiful walnut bed, a tiled bathroom with the spaciousness which indicated high rental. There was a second bedroom which opened on the other side of the bath. There was a kitchen and dining room which opened off the room which Paul Pry entered.

Paul Pry moved through the dining room and into the kitchen.

Then he walked back to the bedroom, turned the flashlight into the closet.

The closet was well filled with clothes of expensive texture. They were feminine garments, and it needed no price tag to show either their quality or their high initial cost.

Paul Pry looked in the bureau drawers and found filmy silk underthings, expensive hose, silk lounging pajamas. He left the bureau and entered the other room. Here he found a closet well crammed with masculine garments. There was a writing desk in this room, and a checkbook in a pigeon hole of the writing desk. Paul Pry took out the checkbook and looked at the stubs.

The stubs were virtually all in a feminine handwriting. They ran to an alarming total.

He was putting the checkbook back in its compartment, when his eye caught a letter with a special-delivery stamp on it. The letter was addressed to Gertrude Fenwick and the address was that of the apartment house. It had been very neatly typewritten and there was no return address on the envelope.

Paul shamelessly inserted his fingers under the flap of the envelope, took out a sheet of typewritten paper and proceeded to read:

My Dear Miss Fenwick:

I dislike very much to involve you in this matter, but I am addressing this communication to you in order that it may reach the eyes of Mr. Charles B. Darwin.

I feel that when Mr. Darwin realizes that even the carefully guarded secret of this apartment is known to the undersigned, he may, perhaps, be more inclined to give heed to my requests.

My last request was turned over to the police, despite the fact that I warned him that such a course would be disastrous. I am now giving him one last chance.

If he will make a check, payable to bearer, to an amount of twenty-five thousand dollars, address it to Fremont Burke, at General Delivery, and make certain that no attempt is made to follow the person who is to receive that letter and cash the check, and in no way seek to trace such a person by marked money or otherwise, and if he will further use his influence to notify his friend, Mr. Perry C. Hammond, that he is making such a remittance, and that he feels it would be well for Mr. Hammond to make such a remittance, then he will be unmolested. The secret of this apartment will remain a secret and he need fear no physical violence from the undersigned.

If, on the other hand, he continues in his course of obstinate refusal to comply with my wishes, if he continues to unite with Mr. Hammond in employing private investigators to seek to learn my identity, his fate and that of Mr. Hammond will be the fate of Mr. Harry Travers.

Very truly yours,
XXXX

The letter was unsigned, except for the diagram of several interlocking "x's" which formed a rude diagram of a cross-stitch, similar to the stitch which had been placed across the lips of the dead body of Harry

Travers, and, later, across those of Charles B. Darwin.

Paul Pry whistled softly when he had read the letter, folded it and thrust it in his pocket. He had directed the beam of the flashlight once more upon the desk, when his ears caught the metallic click of a key being inserted in the lock of the door which led to the corridor.

Paul Pry switched out the flashlight and stood motionless.

He heard the sound of the door open, then closing, and the noise made by the spring lock as it snapped into place. Then he heard the rustle of garments, and the click of a light switch.

Paul Pry slipped the sword cane down from the place where he had it clamped under his arm and moved on furtive feet, stepping noiselessly upon the tiled floor of the bathroom, to where he could look into the bedroom.

There was no one in the bedroom, but a mirror showed him the reflection of the person who had entered the apartment.

She was perhaps twenty-six years of age, slender, well-formed, gray-eyed, blonde, and exceedingly nervous. She had carried two suitcases into the apartment, and the suitcases now reposed on the carpet near her feet, one on either side.

For a moment, Paul Pry saw her reflection in the mirror clearly. Then she moved out of his range of vision, and he suddenly realized she was coming directly toward the bathroom.

He flattened himself in the shadows just back of the door and waited.

The light switch clicked in the bedroom. There was the sound of swift surreptitious movement.

Paul Pry waited for more than a minute. Then, curiosity getting the better of discretion, he peered round the edge of the door.

The young woman had divested herself of her outer garments, and stood attired in filmy underthings, looking at herself in the mirror. As Paul Pry watched, she picked up a dress from the bed, slipped it on, and surveyed the effect.

She nodded to herself with evident approval at what she saw in the mirror, then pulled the dress off over her head.

The dress which she had worn when she entered the apartment, a gray affair which displayed to advantage the curves of her willowy figure, lay upon the bed. Paul Pry waited for her to put it on. Instead, however, she took lingerie from the drawer of the bureau, held it against the satin smoothness of her skin and once more surveyed the reflection with critical inspection.

At length, she picked up the gray dress, slipped it over her head, adjusted it in front of the mirror, then walked rapidly to the living room, where she picked up the suitcases and carried them into the bedroom. She laid the suitcases on the bed, opened them and started folding the garments into them.

Paul Pry, watching from his place of concealment, saw that the suitcases had been empty when she took them into the room; that she carefully folded the gowns, packing the cases as tightly as possible; that she also put in the elaborately embroidered silk lingerie which she had taken from the bureau drawer.

When both cases had been packed to the point of bursting with the most modish of gowns, the most expensive selection of underthings and accessories, the young woman struggled with the straps, trying to get the suitcases closed.

It was at that moment that Paul Pry, his

sword cane held under his arm, his hat in his hand, stepped into the bedroom.

"I beg your pardon," he said.

She gave a sudden scream, jumped back from the bed and stared at him with wide, startled eyes.

Paul Pry bowed courteously. "I happened," he explained, "to be in the bathroom. I couldn't help watching you. Perhaps it is a 'Peeping Tom' complex that I have. I didn't know I possessed it until just this moment, but you were beautiful, and I was curious. Need more be said?"

She was white to the lips. She stared at him wordlessly.

"But," Paul Pry went on, "having been permitted to invade the privacy of milady's boudoir, I recognized the obligations which are incident to the benefits. Apparently you need someone to assist you in closing the suitcases. May I offer my services?"

Words came chokingly from her lips.

"Who . . . who . . . who are you, and what do you want?"

"The name," he said, "really doesn't matter, I assure you. It doesn't matter in the slightest. When people get acquainted under such charmingly informal circumstances, I think names have but little to do with it. Suppose, therefore, that I shall call you Gertrude, and you call me Paul?"

"But," she said with swift alarm, "my name is not Gertrude."

"No?" he asked.

"No," she said. "my name is—"

"Yes, yes," he told her, "go on. Only the first name, if you please. I am not interested in last names."

"The name," she said, "is Thelma."

"A remarkably pretty name," he told her. "And may I ask, Thelma, what are you doing in this apartment?"

"I was getting some clothes," she said.

"Your clothes?" he asked.

"Of course."

"Then," he said, "you must be aware of the untimely death of the person who is maintaining this establishment."

"No! No!" she said. "I don't know anything about that. In fact, I don't know anything about the place at all."

"You just left your clothes here?" he asked.

"Yes," she said. "I'd just moved in. You see, I subleased the apartment."

"From whom?" he inquired.

"From an agent," she said.

He laughed. "Come, come," he said, "you'll have to do better than that. Let's be frank with each other. This apartment was maintained by Charles B. Darwin. Darwin recently met a very violent end. You have doubtless heard of the death of Harry Travers. The circumstances surrounding the death of Darwin were almost identical. The lips, if I may be pardoned for speaking of such a gruesome matter, were sewed tightly shut with a peculiar cross-stitch. Now, it is quite apparent that a person who sews lips of a man, does so with some motive. Were the man living, that motive might well be to insure temporary silence. But there are much better and less painful methods of insuring silence. To sew the lips of a dead man had nothing whatever to do with the powers of speech. One would judge, therefore, that the sewing of the lips was either by way of warning to others, or as a gesture, to make the murder seem the more gruesome. It might also well be a warning to to others who had been approached along certain lines not to communicate the facts to the police."

She swayed slightly.

"You're faint?" he asked. "Do sit down in one of these chairs."

She shook her head in tense silence. "No," she said, "I'm all right. I'm going to tell you the truth."

"I wish you would, Thelma," he said.

"I'm a model," she said, "in a dressmaking establishment. I know the lady by sight who accompanied Mr. Darwin when these dresses were purchased. I happened to meet her on the street just an hour or so ago. She told me that owing to circumstances over which she had no control, she was leaving the city at once; that she had left a very fine wardrobe here, and that she knew the dresses would fit me, because we were almost identical in size. She gave me a key to the apartment, and told me to come up and take whatever I wanted."

"Why didn't you bring a trunk?" asked Paul Pry.

"Because," she said, "I didn't want too many clothes; I just wanted some of the pretty things that would give me a break."

"And she gave you her key to the apartment."

"Yes."

"Is it at all possible," Paul Pry inquired, "that you are, perhaps, drawing upon your imagination?"

She shook her head.

"And you're not the young woman who occupied this apartment?"

"You should be able to figure that one out for yourself," she said. "You stood there and watched me trying on the things." She lowered her eyes.

"Are you, perhaps," asked Paul Pry, "trying to blush?"

Her eyes flashed with swift emotion. "You should be ashamed of yourself," she said, "standing there and watching a woman dress that way!"

Paul Pry bowed his head humbly. "Please accept my most profound apologies," he said. "And would you, perhaps, let me see the key with which you entered the apartment?"

She inserted her fingers into a small pocket in her dress, took out a key, started to hand it to him, then stopped suddenly.

Paul Pry's eyes were hard and insistent. "The key," he said.

"I don't know who you are," she said, "and I don't know what right you've got to ask for the key."

Paul Pry moved toward her. His eyes were cold and hypnotic. "The key," he repeated.

She stared into his eyes for several seconds, then slowly opened her hand.

The key dropped to the carpet.

Paul Pry stooped to pick it up.

At the moment she moved with swift speed. Paul Pry swung himself to one side and dodged as a small, pearl-handled automatic glittered in her hand. "Stick them up!" she said savagely.

Paul Pry lunged forward, caught her about the knees. She gave a half scream and fell forward, the gun dropping from her hand. They came together on the floor, a tangled mass of arms and legs, from which Paul Pry emerged presently, smiling and debonair.

"Naughty, naughty," he said. "I really should spank you for that."

He took the automatic and slipped it into his hip pocket. Then, as the young woman sat on the floor arranging her clothes so as to cover her legs, Paul Pry searched until he found the key, held it up and smiled knowingly.

"I thought so," he said. "A skeleton key."

She stared at him wordlessly.

"You are," said Paul Pry, "in the eyes of the law, a burglar, a person guilty of making a felonious entrance and taking property which does not belong to you."

She said nothing.

"Under the circumstances," said Paul Pry, striding easily across the room, "I think I will have to telephone to the police."

She remained as he had left her—motionless, silent, and with a face which was drained of expression.

Paul Pry approached the door which led into the corridor, turned and smiled. "Upon second thought, however," he said, "in view of the most charming display of feminine pulchritude which you unwittingly gave me, I am going to let mercy temper justice."

With a swift motion of his arms and hands, he flipped back the spring catch on the door, pulled the door open, stepped into the corridor and slammed the door behind him.

There was no sound of pursuit, no commotion. The apartment remained completely silent.

3

The Wooden Fish

Paul Pry was faultlessly attired in evening clothes when he pressed the doorbell of the magnificent residence of Perry C. Hammond.

A dour-visaged butler opened the door. Pry met his sour look with a disarming smile.

"A gentleman," he said, "who refuses to divulge his name, wishes to see Mr. Hammond at once upon a matter of the most urgent nature."

"Mr. Hammond, sir," said the butler, "is not at home."

"You will explain to Mr. Hammond," said Paul Pry, still smiling, "that I am a specialist in my line."

"Mr. Hammond, sir, is not at home."

"Quite right, my man, quite right. And, will you please add to the explanation you make to Mr. Hammond that my particular specialty is in disorders of the lips—disorders which have to do with a permanent

195

silence, brought about through mechanical means."

Paul Pry's smiling eyes locked with those of the butler, and suddenly the smile left Paul Pry's eyes. His face became cold and stern.

"You will," he said, "convey that message to Mr. Hammond immediately. Otherwise, I will communicate with Mr. Hammond in some other way, and explain to him the reason my message was not delivered personally. I don't mind assuring you that Mr. Hammond will consider you have committed a major indiscretion."

The butler hesitated for a long moment. "Will you step this way, sir?" he asked.

He ushered Paul Pry through a reception hallway, into a small entrance parlor. "Please be seated, sir," he said. "I will see if, perhaps, Mr. Hammond has returned."

The butler glided from the room, and the door had no sooner closed upon him, than Paul Pry, moving with noiseless stealth, jerked open the door and stepped once more into the reception corridor.

His quick eyes had detected a small enameled box for out-going mail, and Paul Pry's deft fingers raised the lid of the box and explored the interior.

There were three letters addressed in a cramped, angular handwriting. Paul Pry flipped the letters, one over the other, in rapid succession, scanning the addresses. The third envelope was addressed to Fremont Burke, General Delivery.

Paul Pry stuck it in his pocket, returned the others to the mail box, and then moved on furtive feet back into the reception parlor.

He had barely resumed his seat when the butler entered through another door. "Mr. Hammond," he said, "will see you."

Paul Pry walked across the room, followed the butler down a passageway and went through a door the servant indicated.

A man with great puffs under his eyes, a look of infinite weariness upon his face, stared at him with expressionless interrogation. "Well," he said, "what was it you wanted?"

"I have reason," said Paul Pry, "to believe that your life is in danger."

"I think you are mistaken," said Hammond.

"I have reason," said Paul Pry, "to believe that the same fate which overtook Charles C. Darwin may, perhaps, be in store for you."

Perry Hammond shook his head. "Whoever gave you your information," he said, "misinformed you."

"In other words," said Paul Pry slowly, "you deny that you have received any demands from a person who has threatened you with death or disaster in the event you fail to comply? You deny that you have been threatened with death, under circumstances similar to the threats which were made to Mr. Charles Darwin?"

"I," said Perry Hammond, slowly and deliberately, "don't know what you're talking about. I saw you because I thought you might be interested in getting some information about Mr. Darwin. As far as I am concerned, you can get out and stay out."

Paul Pry bowed. "Thank you very much," he said, "for your interview, Mr. Hammond." He turned on his heel.

"Wait a minute," said the millionaire in a cold, husky voice.

"Are you a newspaper reporter?"

"No," said Paul Pry without turning.

"Then who the devil are you?" asked Hammond with sudden irritation.

Paul Pry turned to face the millionaire. "I am a man," he said, smiling affably, "who is going to make you extremely sorry you lied to him."

With that, he turned once more and strode steadily and purposefully down the carpeted corridor.

Mugs Magoo looked up from his whiskey glass as Paul Pry latchkeyed the apartment door. "Well," he said mournfully, "I see you're still with us."

"Temporarily, at least, Mugs," Paul Pry retorted, smiling.

He hung up his hat and coat, crossed to a closet and opened the door. The closet contained a collection of drums, drums of various sorts and descriptions.

Mugs Magoo shuddered. "For God's sake," he said, "don't start that!"

Paul Pry laughed lightly and fingered the drums with the attentive care that a hunter might give to the selection of a gun from a gun cabinet.

Mugs Magoo hastily poured liquor into the glass. "At least," he said, "give me fifteen minutes to get liquored before you start. Those damn drums do things to me. They get into my blood and make the pulses pound."

Paul Pry's voice was almost dreamy as he

picked out a round piece of wood which seemed to be entirely solid, save for a cut along one end, with two holes bored at the end of the cut.

"That, Mugs," he said, "is the function of drums. We don't know exactly what it is they do, but they seem to get into a person's blood. You don't like the sound of drums, Mugs, because you are afraid of the primitive. You are continually trying to run away from yourself. Doubtless a psycho-analyst could look into your past and find that your taste for whiskey had its inception in an attempt to drown some real or fancied sorrow."

Mugs Magoo let his face show extreme consternation. "You're not going to take me to one of those psycho-analysts?" he asked.

Paul Pry shook his head. "Certainly not, Mugs," he said. "I think it is too late to effect a cure now, and, in the event a cure was effected, Mugs, you would lose your taste for whiskey.

"Drums, Mugs, do to me exactly what whiskey does to you. If you could cultivate a taste for drums, I think I would endeavor to cure you of the whiskey habit. But, since you cannot, the only thing I can do is to let you enjoy your pleasures in your own way, and insist that you allow me an equal latitude."

Paul Pry sat down in the chair which faced the big fireplace, took a long, slender stick, to the end of which had been affixed a rose-bud-shaped bit of hard wood.

"Now, Mugs," he said, "here we have a *Mok Yeitt,* otherwise known as a 'wooden fish.' The wooden fish is a prayer drum used by the Buddhists in China to pave the way for a friendly reception to their prayers. If you will listen, Mugs, you will get the remarkable delicacy of tone which the better specimens of these drums give. They are cunningly carved by hand. A hole is made in either end of the slit, and the wood is hollowed out with painstaking care . . ."

"For God's sake!" said Mugs Magoo, "don't! You're going to drive me crazy with that thing!"

Paul Pry shook his head, started tapping the wooden stick against the bulge of the drum. A throbbing sound filled the apartment, a sound which had a peculiar wooden resonance which trailed off into vibrating overtones.

Mugs Magoo frantically downed the whiskey, poured himself another drink, gulped it, then shivered and sat motionless. After a moment, he placed his one hand against his ear.

"I can shut out half of the sound, anyhow," he said, at length.

Paul Pry paid no attention to him, but continued tapping upon the drum at regular intervals.

"What's the idea of all the drumming now?" asked Mugs Magoo.

"I'm trying to concentrate," said Paul Pry. "I think I almost have the solution I want."

Abruptly, he ceased drumming and smiled benignly at Mugs. "Yes, Mugs," he said, "I have the solution."

Mugs Magoo shivered. "It'll be another five minutes," he said, "before that whiskey takes effect. I was spared five minutes of torture anyway. What is the solution?"

Paul Pry set down the *Mok Yeitt*. He reached into the inside pocket of his coat, pulled out an envelope, the flap of which had been steamed open, and took out a letter and a tinted oblong of paper.

"Mugs," he said, "I have here a letter bearing the angular signature of Perry C. Hammond, a multi-millionaire. Let me read it to you.

"Mr. Fremont Burke,
General Delivery,
    City.
Dear Mr. Burke:
    I herewith comply with your request. You will find enclosed my check for twenty-five thousand dollars, payable to bearer. I wish to assure you that no attempt whatever will be made to interfere with the cashing of that check. On the other hand, I have notified my bankers by telephone that the check represents the transfer of consideration in a bona fide business deal, and that they are to promptly honor the check when it is presented.

    Trusting that this complies in full with your demands and that I may now be at liberty to consider the matter closed, I am,

Very truly yours,
Perry C. Hammond.

Mugs Magoo stared at Paul Pry. "A check," he said, "for twenty-five thousand dollars?"

Paul Pry nodded. "And don't forget, Mugs," he said, "that it's payable to bearer."

"But," said Mugs Magoo, "who is the bearer?"

Paul Pry got to his feet, replaced the wooden fish in the drum closet, closed the door, turned to Mugs and smiled once more. "Mugs," he said, "I am the bearer."

Mugs Magoo stared at him with eyes that seemed to pop from his head. "My God!" he said. "You've been mixing into things again! You're going to have the police after you for theft, Perry Hammond after you for fraud, and probably the man who pulls the cross-stitch murders after you, hammer and tongs, trying to kill you and sew your lips up!"

Paul Pry pursed his lips thoughtfully, then nodded his head.

"Yes, Mugs," he said, "I should say that that is a very fair statement of the probable consequences. In fact, I would say that it is a somewhat conservative estimate."

Smiling, he crossed to the writing desk and pulled down the slab of heavy wood which served as a writing table. He explored the pigeon holes which were disclosed in the back of the desk.

"You will remember, Mugs," he said, "that at one time I secured a long, purple envelope, with a red border. You asked me what the devil I wanted with such an envelope, and I told you that I was keeping it because it was distinctive."

Mugs Magoo nodded. "Yes," he said, "I remember that."

Paul Pry took a fountain pen from his pocket and addressed the purple envelope with the red border.

"Mr. Fremont Burke, General Delivery, City," he said when he had finished writing. "The red ink shows up rather to advantage on that purple background. It makes it quite harmonious."

"What's in the envelope?" asked Mugs Magoo.

"Nothing," said Paul Pry.

"What's going to be in it?"

"Nothing."

"What's the idea?" asked Mugs Magoo.

Paul Pry smiled. He took from another compartment of the desk a stamped envelope. He addressed that envelope also to Fremont Burke, General Delivery, City.

"What's going in that envelope?" asked Mugs Magoo.

"In this envelope," said Paul Pry, smiling, "is going the best forgery of this check which I can make, and I'm satisfied, Mugs, that it will be quite a clever forgery."

Mugs Magoo stared at Paul Pry in wordless contemplation. Then, "You're going to cash the original check?" he asked.

Paul Pry nodded.

"How about the forged check?" asked Mugs Magoo.

Paul Pry shrugged his shoulders. "That, Mugs," he said, "is a matter which lies between the bank and the man who presents the check."

"But," said Mugs Magoo, "suppose the forged check should be presented first?"

Paul Pry smiled patronizingly. "Come, come, Mugs," he said, "you must give me credit for a little intelligence. The original check will be cashed before the forged check ever reaches the post office."

"And what," asked Mugs Magoo, "is the idea of the two letters—one in the colored envelope and one in the plain envelope?"

"That, Mugs," said Paul Pry, "comes under that classification of a trade secret. Really, it's something that I can't tell you unless you permit me to do a little more drumming."

Mugs Magoo shook his head violently from side to side in extreme agitation.

"What's the idea of the shake?" asked Paul Pry.

"I wanted to see if the whiskey had taken effect," said Mugs Magoo. "If it had, I'd let you drum some more, but I see that I either didn't get enough whiskey, or else I misjudged the time it would take to make me dizzy. I can't stand the drumming, so you can keep your damned trade secret to yourself."

Paul Pry chuckled and thrust the envelopes into his inside pocket. "Tomorrow at this time, Mugs, I'll be twenty-five thousand dollars richer. Moreover, I'll be embarked upon an interesting adventure."

"Tomorrow at this time," said Mugs Magoo, with solemn melancholy, "you'll be stretched out on a marble slab, and a coroner and an autopsy surgeon will be staring at the cross-stitches that are placed across your lips."

—4—

The Second Check

Paul Pry, wearing an overcoat which was turned up around the neck, a felt hat which was pulled down low over his forehead, and with heavily smoked glasses shielding his eyes, shoved the check through the cashier's window.

The cashier stared at Paul Pry's smoked glasses, looked at the check, said, "Just a moment," and stepped from his grilled cage. He consulted a memorandum, looked at the check once more, sighed, and, with obvious reluctance, picked up a sheaf of currency.

"How," he asked, "would you like to have this?"

"In hundreds," said Paul Pry, "if that's convenient."

The cashier counted out hundred dollar bills in lots of ten, stacked them all together and snapped a large elastic band about them.

"You'll take them that way?" he asked.

"Yes."

"You wish to count them?"

"No," said Paul Pry, and turned away.

His long overcoat flapped about his ankles as he walked. He could feel the gaze of the cashier striking between his shoulder blades with almost physical impact.

Paul Pry went at once to the post office, where he dropped the two letters through the slot marked for city mail. Then he went out to lunch, and, after lunch, he strolled back to the post office.

He managed to stand where, without seeming to be too conspicuous, he could watch the window marked "General Delivery—A to G."

Shortly after two-thirty, a young woman, stylishly gowned, presented herself at the window.

Paul Pry, standing some thirty feet away, at the end of a corridor, saw the clerk at the general-delivery window hand out a long envelope of purple tint, with a red border. The young woman took it, looked at it curiously. A moment later, the man behind the grill slid another envelope through the window. The girl took it, stared curiously at both envelopes. A moment later she moved away from the window, paused to open the envelopes, staring with puzzled countenance at the empty interior of the purple envelope.

Evidently she expected the check which was in the second envelope, for, as she removed the slip of paper, a look of relief came over her features. Paul Pry, standing where he could observe her every move, saw that she was laboring under great tension. Her lips seemed inclined to quiver, and her hands shook as she crumpled the purple envelope, held it over the huge iron waste basket as though to drop it. Then, apparently she thought better of it, for she uncrumpled the envelope, folded it and thrust it in her purse.

She walked from the post-office building, down the granite steps to the sidewalk, where a second young woman was waiting in an automobile.

Paul Pry, following behind, yet careful lest he should seem too eager, was unable to get a clear view of the woman who drove the automobile. But he saw the young woman who had taken the letters from the post office jump into the car. The car immediately drove off at high speed.

Paul Pry ran down the post-office steps to the lot where he had left his own automobile parked. He started the motor, then divested himself of the overcoat, the dark glasses, and shifted the slouch hat for one with a stiffer brim, letting the engine of his car warm up as he was making the changes. Then he stepped into the machine, drove at once to the bank where he had cashed the twenty-five thousand dollar check earlier in the day.

He made no effort to find a legitimate parking place for his car, but left it in front of a fire plug, certain that he would receive a tag, certain, also, that the car would be located in an advantageous position when he wished to use it once more.

He walked through the revolving door, stood in the ornate marble foyer looking at the long corridors with their grilled windows, the desks of executives, the customers crowding about the stand on which counter checks and deposit slips were kept.

Paul Pry went at once to the end of the longest line he could see, stood there fumbling a deposit slip in his fingers.

He had been there less than five seconds when he saw the young woman who had taken the letter from the post office walk with quick, nervous steps to the window of the paying teller. She presented a check and was promptly referred to the cashier. Paul Pry watched her as she thrust the check through the window to the cashier, saw the hand of the cashier as it took the check and turned it over and over while he studied it intently.

A moment later, there was the faint sound of an electric buzzer. A uniformed officer who had been loitering about, watching the patrons idly, suddenly stiffened to attention, looked about him, caught a signal from the cashier. He moved unostentatiously forward.

During all of this time the young woman had stood at the window, apparently entirely oblivious of what was taking place about her.

Paul Pry walked to the telephone booths, dropped a nickel and called the number of Perry C. Hammond.

A moment later, a feminine voice announced that Mr. Hammond's secretary was speaking, and Paul Pry stated that he desired to speak with Mr. Hammond concerning the matter of a twenty-five thousand dollar check which had been issued to Fremont Burke.

Almost at once he heard the sound of whispers, and then Hammond's voice came over the wire, a voice which was dry with nervousness, despite the millionaire's attempt to make it sound casual.

"How are you this afternoon, Mr. Hammond?" said Paul Pry cordially.

"What was it you wanted to talk to me about?" asked the millionaire.

"Oh," said Paul Pry casually, "I just

wanted to advise you that I had stolen twenty-five thousand dollars from you and that I trusted the loss wouldn't inconvenience you in any way."

"That you had what?" screamed the millionaire.

"Stolen twenty-five thousand dollars from you," Paul Pry remarked. "I don't think that there's any occasion to get excited over it. From all I hear, you can well afford to spare it. But I didn't want you to be embarrassed on account of the theft."

"What are you talking about?" Hammond demanded.

"Merely," said Paul Pry, "that my name happens to be Fremont Burke. I was flat broke and had tried to get five dollars from my brother in Denver. I called at the post office to see if there was any mail for me, and a letter was delivered to me. I opened it and saw there was a check enclosed for twenty-five thousand dollars, payable to bearer.

"Naturally, I thought the thing was some sort of a joke, but thought perhaps I might be able to get the price of a meal out of it, so I took it to the bank. To my surprise, they cashed it at once and without question. I realized then, of course, that I had, fortunately, stumbled on a remittance which was intended for someone else. Not wishing to disappoint the someone else, I forged your name to a check, put it in an envelope and mailed it to Fremont Burke, in care of General Delivery."

The millionaire's voice was almost a scream of terror.

"You did what?" he shrieked.

"Come, come," said Paul Pry. "There's no need of so much excitement. I forged your check for twenty-five thousand dollars and put it in the mail. It occurred to me that the person who received that check might have been expecting a legitimate business remittance from you, and would probably put the check through his bank for collection, or might possibly present the check at the cashier's window.

"Under the circumstances, the check would probably be branded as a forgery. I did my best to make the forgery a good one, but, you understand, even a large bank will look carefully at a second check for twenty-five thousand dollars, payable to bearer, which is presented in the course of one business day.

"It occurs to me, therefore, that if the bank should advise you someone has forged a check and is presenting it for collection, it might be advisable for you to refuse to prosecute that person on the ground of forgery. You see, he might be acting in perfect good faith, and . . ."

There was an inarticulate exclamation at the other end of the line, followed by the slamming of a receiver on the hook. Paul Pry figured that Perry Hammond had cut off the connection in order to rush through a call to the bank.

He strolled from the telephone booth, walked across to a desk, filled out a deposit slip and strolled to the window which was nearest to the cashier's window.

The uniformed officer had moved up and taken the young woman by the arm. She was white-faced and trembling.

"I tell you," Paul Pry heard her say, "I know nothing whatever about it, except that I was hired to get this check out of the mail and cash it. After I had the money I was supposed to call a certain telephone number, and I would then be given instructions as to how I should proceed. That's all I know about it."

The telephone at the cashier's elbow rang sharply and insistently. The cashier picked up the telephone, said, "hello," and then let surprise register on his countenance. After a moment he said: "Yes, Mr. Hammond, late this morning. I remembered particularly that you had left instructions about the matter, and . . ."

The receiver made squawking, metallic noises which were inaudible to Paul Pry's ears, but the face of the cashier flushed with color.

"Just a minute," he said. "I think you're nervous and excited, Mr. Hammond. If you'll just . . ."

He was interrupted by more squawking noises from the receiver.

The line at which Paul Pry had been standing moved up, so that Paul Pry found himself at the window.

"I wish to make a deposit," he said, thrusting the deposit slip through the window, together with ten of the one-hundred-dollar bills he had received from the bank earlier in the day.

The man at the window was smiling and affable. "You should go down to the fourth window," he said, "the one marked 'Deposits—M to R'."

Paul Pry looked apologetic and embarrassed.

"Just right down there where you see the lettering over the window," said the man, smiling unctuously.

Paul Pry walked slowly past the cashier's window. He was in time to hear the cashier say to the officer: "It's quite all right, Madson. We can't cash this check because the signature is irregular; but Mr. Hammond promises that he will rectify the matter, so far as Mr. Burke is concerned. It seems there's been a very serious mistake, for which the bank is in no way responsible. It's due to the carelessness of a customer in mailing checks payable to bearer . . ."

There was more, which Paul Pry could not hear because it was delivered in a lower voice, a voice which was almost surreptitiously confidential, and because appearances required that Paul Pry should move over toward the window which had been pointed out to him.

He did, however, see the young lady move away from the window, in the direction of the telephone booths. She dropped a coin and called a number. She talked rapidly and excitedly, then paused to listen for several seconds, at the end of which time she nodded her head and hung up the telephone.

Paul Pry followed her from the bank, down to the curb, where he saw the same car which he had seen parked in front of the post office. The young woman got into the car, which at once drove off.

This time, Paul Pry's car was parked where he had no difficulty in getting into an advantageous position directly behind the coupe which he was trailing. He ripped the red police tag from the steering wheel, thrust it in his pocket, and concentrated his attention upon following the car ahead.

It was not a particularly easy task. The young woman in the car ahead was a good driver, and she was evidently going some place in very much of a hurry.

The car stopped, at length, in front of a building which apparently housed a speak-easy. The young woman left the car, walked across the curb with rapid, nervous steps, rang a bell and stood perfectly still while a panel slid back in the door and a face regarded her.

A moment later, the door opened, and the young woman vanished.

The coupe left the curb, and, as it sped away, the driver turned for one last look at the door where the young woman had been admitted.

Paul Pry started nervously as he saw the face pressed against the glass in the rear window of the coupe. It was the face of the young woman he had met previously in the apartment which Charles B. Darwin had maintained so secretly, the young woman who had been trying on clothes in front of the mirror. However, it was too late then to do anything about it. The coupe continued on its way, and Paul Pry began to put into operation a certain very definite plan he had in mind.

—5—

Cross-Stitch Killer

There was a drug store across the street, and Paul Pry stepped across to it, purchased a woman's purse, a lip stick, compact, handkerchief, a package of chewing gum. He paid for the purchases with one of the hundred-dollar bills he had received, and thrust the change into the purse. He also folded two more of the hundred-dollar bills and pushed them into the purse. The drug clerk watched him curiously, but said nothing.

Paul Pry walked back across the street to the speakeasy. He rang the bell and a panel slid back.

"About four or five minutes ago," said Paul Pry, "there was a young woman, a brunette, wearing a blue skirt and a small, tight-fitting, blue hat. She got out of a coupe and came in here."

"What about it?" said the frosty voice of the man who regarded Paul Pry with hostile eyes through the wicket in the doorway.

"I've got to see her," said Paul Pry.

"You got a card?"

"No. But I've got to see that young woman."

"You can't see her."

Paul Pry fidgeted. "You see," he said, "she dropped her purse. I picked it up and intended to return it to her. Then I looked inside of it and saw what was in it, and the temptation was too much for me. I started to run away with it. You see, I've got a wife and a couple of kiddies who haven't had anything much to eat for two or three days now. I've been out of work and my savings are completely used up. I had to do anything I could to get by. When I saw the money in this purse, I decided I wouldn't return the purse. Then, after I'd walked half a block, I realized I couldn't steal, so I had to bring it to her."

"All right," said the man, "give me the purse and I'll take it to her."

Paul Pry opened the purse. "Look," he said, "there's almost three hundred dollars in it."

"I'll take it to her," said the man in the doorway.

"Like hell you will," said Paul Pry. "She'll probably give me a five spot, or perhaps a ten, or she might even get generous and give me a twenty. That would mean a lot to me. I couldn't take the purse, but I sure as hell could take a reward."

"If she wants to give you a reward, I'll bring it to you," said the man.

Paul Pry's laugh was mocking and scornful.

The man on the other side of the door seemed undecided.

"You either let me in and I take it to her personally," said Paul Pry, "or she doesn't get it. If you want to keep a customer from getting her purse back, it's all right by me; I've done my duty in trying to return it. If you won't let her have it, I'll put an ad in the paper telling the whole circumstances."

"Look here," said the man who glowered

through the opening in the doorway, "this is a high-class restaurant. We put on a floor show, and the young woman who just came in is one of the girls who works in the floor show. Now you've got that purse and it belongs to her. If you try to take it away, I'll call a cop and have you arrested."

Paul Pry sneered. "A fat chance you've got of calling a cop," he said. "I'd raise a commotion and tell the whole cockeyed world that this place was a speakeasy; that I was trying to get in to return the purse and you wouldn't let me in, but started calling a cop. If you're a respectable restaurant why the hell don't you open your door so the public can patronize you?"

The bolts slipped back in the door.

"Oh hell," said the man, "come on in and get it over with. You're just one of those damn pests that show up every so often."

"Where do I find her?" asked Paul Pry.

"The name is Ellen Tracy. She's in one of the dressing rooms up on the second floor. I'll have one of the waiters take you up."

"And want to chisel in on the reward," said Paul Pry. "Not much you don't. I'm on my way right now."

He pushed past the man and ran up the stairs.

There was a telephone at the man's elbow. As Paul Pry was halfway up the stairs he heard the telephone ring, heard the man answer it and then lower his voice to a mere confidential mumble.

Paul Pry would have given much to have heard that conversation, but he had no time to wait. With his sword cane grasped firmly in his hand, he took the stairs two at a time. He walked rapidly across a dance floor, pushed his way through a curtained doorway, walked up a flight of steps. He saw a row of doors, one with the name "Ellen Tracy" painted on it. He tapped with his knuckles.

"Who is it?" called a woman's voice.

"A package for you," said Paul Pry.

The door opened a few inches. A woman's hand and bare arm protruded. "Give it to me," she said.

Paul Pry pushed the door open.

She fell back with a little scream.

She had slipped out of her dress and was attired in underwear, shoes and stockings. There was a costume on a stool beside a dressing table and a kimono draped carelessly over a chair. The young woman made no attempt to pick up the kimono, but stood staring at Paul Pry, apparently entirely unconscious of her apparel.

"Well," she said, "what's the big idea?"

"Listen," said Paul Pry, "I came from him—the man who got you to get that check from the post office. You know what I mean."

Her face was suddenly drained of color, her eyes dark with alarm. "Yes," she said in a low, half-choked voice.

"What did they tell you at the bank?" said Paul Pry. "It's important as hell."

"Mr. Hammond," she said, "said that he would make the check right. He wanted the bank to cash it, but they wouldn't cash a forged check. He said that he'd make the check good. I telephoned a few minutes ago and explained the whole thing. You should have known."

"There's some question about that," Paul Pry said. "You telephoned to the wrong number. Somebody else seems to have got the information. Are you sure you telephoned to the right number?"

There was a puzzled frown on her forehead. She nodded slowly.

"What was the number?" asked Paul Pry.

She fell back from him suddenly, as though he had struck her. Her face was deathly white. She seemed to shrink within herself. "Who . . . who . . . who are you?" she asked in a voice which was shrill with panic.

"I told you who I am," Paul Pry said.

She shook her head slowly. Her eyes were wide and dark. "Get out of here!" she said in a half whisper. "For God's sake get out of here while there's still time!"

Paul Pry took a step toward her. "Listen," he said, "you either know what you're mixed up in or you don't. In any event . . ."

A woman's scream, shrill and high-pitched, interrupted his sentence. The scream seemed to come from one of the adjoining dressing rooms.

Paul Pry stood still, listening, his eyes slitted, his mouth a thin, straight line. The scream rang out again, louder and more insistent.

Paul Pry stared at the woman. "Who's that screaming?" he asked.

She could hardly answer, so great was her terror. Her tongue clung to the roof of her mouth. Her throat seemed paralyzed. At length, she stammered: "It's Thelma . . . that's her room next to mine."

"Thelma?" asked Paul Pry.

She nodded.

"Tell me," said Paul Pry, "was that the girl who drove the coupe that took you to the post office and the bank?"

She nodded once more.

Paul Pry jabbed his finger at her as though he had been stabbing her with a weapon. "You," he said, "stay right there. Don't you make a move. Don't try to go out. Don't let anyone else in. When I come back you let me in. Do you understand?"

She nodded.

Paul jerked the door open.

The scream from the adjoining dressing room sounded once more as Paul Pry jumped through the doorway into the corridor, and flung himself at the door of the next dressing room.

The door was unlocked.

Paul Pry pushed his way into the dressing room, then, at what he saw, kicked the door shut behind him.

The young woman who had given him the name Thelma when he had caught her trying on clothes in the millionaire's apartment, was standing in the far corner of the room. Her waist was torn open at the throat, ripped for its entire length. The brassiere was pulled down from her shoulders. Her hair was in disarray. Her skirt was lying on a chair. Her step-ins were torn in two or three places. She held a gun in her right hand. As Paul Pry kicked the door shut, she screamed again.

Paul Pry stared at her and at the gun.

"O.K., Thelma," he said. "What's the trouble? Quick!"

She swayed toward him. "C-c-c-can't you see?" she said.

"I can see plenty," he told her, looking at the white of the girl's skin, a white which showed angry red places where, apparently, blows had been rained.

"Did you see the man who went out of here?" she asked.

Paul Pry shook his head. He was staring at her with eyes narrowed.

"I c-c-c-can't tell you," she said. "Come over here and let me w-w-w-whisper to you. It was awful!"

Paul Pry moved toward her.

She shivered. "I'm c-c-c-cold," she said. "I'm going to faint. Take off your coat and put it around me. I'm so c-c-c-cold. Put

227

your coat around my shoulders." She swayed toward him.

Paul Pry jumped forward and caught her by the shoulders. He spun her abruptly, brutally, jerking the gun from her hand as he did so.

She staggered halfway across the small dressing room, dropped to a chair and sat staring at Paul Pry with startled eyes.

"All right," said Paul Pry, "now give me the lowdown and do it quick!"

"How did you know?" she asked.

"It was too raw," he told her. "Give me the lowdown."

"I don't think I could have gone through with it anyway," she said. "But my life depended on it."

"All right," he said, "I think I know the answer, but tell me what it was."

"I saw that you were following us," she said. "I recognized you. I telephoned the information to the party to whom I make my reports. He told me to rush up to my dressing room, pull my clothes off, make it look as though I had been attacked, and scream. When you came in, I was to shoot. He gave me the gun, but he didn't trust me. He only gave me one shell in the gun. I was to fire that one shell when you were so close

I couldn't miss. When he heard the shot, he was to come in. I was to swear that you had tried to attack me."

"Then what?" asked Paul Pry.

"That's all," she said, "if the sound of the shot attracted any attention. If it didn't, I wasn't going to figure in it. I wasn't going to have to say anything. He was going to dispose of your body some way; I don't know how. All I had to do was to pack up my things and take a long trip around the world. He was going to give me the tickets and everything."

"And if you didn't do it?" asked Paul Pry.

"Then," she said, "neither one of us was to come out of here alive."

"You know of the murderous activities of this man you're working for?" asked Paul Pry.

She hesitated a moment, then nodded her head. "Yes," she said slowly, "I know now. I didn't until a few minutes ago."

"And," said Paul Pry, "he's here in this restaurant?"

"He owns the place," she said.

Paul Pry flipped open the cylinder of the gun. It was as the young woman had said —there was but one shell in it.

Paul Pry pushed the cylinder back into position. "Let's get out," he said.

She shook her head. "You can't do it," she said. "He's waiting outside, and he's got another man with him. They're going to kill us both unless I go through with what he told me to do."

"Suppose no one from the outside hears the shot?" said Paul Pry. "Then what?"

"Then," she said, "I think . . ."

"Go on," he told her, as her voice trailed away into silence, "tell me what you think."

Her voice came in a whisper. "I think," she said, "he's going to sew up your lips and dump your body somewhere."

She shuddered and trembled as though with a chill.

Paul Pry stood in front of her, staring at her with level, appraising eyes. "Look here, Thelma," he said, "if you're lying to me it's going to mean your life. Tell me the truth. If no one hears the shot, he's going to dispose of my body that way?"

She nodded, then said, after a minute, in a dull, hopeless tone: "But it's no use now. We're both going to die. You don't know him. You don't know how absolutely, unutterably ruthless, how unspeakably cruel . . ."

Paul Pry moved swiftly. He took the dressing table, tilted it to a sharp angle, pulled open one of the drawers, inserted the revolver and pulled the trigger.

The gun gave forth a muffled *boom*.

Paul Pry toppled the dressing table to the floor. It fell with a bang which shook the walls.

Paul Pry, stepping back, tossed the useless gun to the floor, took the razor-keen blade of his sword cane from its scabbard, held himself flat against the wall, just to one side of the door, so that the opening door would serve to conceal him from who entered the room.

There was a period of silence.

Thelma put her head in her hands and started to cry.

Slowly, the knob on the door rattled into motion. The latch clicked; the door opened slowly. Two men entered the room. Paul Pry could hear the sounds of their shuffling feet, but could not see them.

A masculine voice said: "Where is he, Thelma?"

The sobbing girl said nothing, but kept her face in her hands, sobbing hopelessly.

The men moved further into the room. One of them walked toward her.

Paul Pry took a deep breath and kicked the door shut.

Two pairs of startled eyes stared at him. One of the men was the man who had been on guard at the door of the speakeasy. The other was a man Paul Pry had never seen before—a well-dressed man with curly, black hair, eyes that glinted with dark fire. He had a saturnine cast to his countenance, and his face seemed to radiate a sort of hypnotic power.

Both men had guns which dangled from their hands.

The man who had guarded the door of the speakeasy was nearest to Paul Pry. He raised his gun.

Paul Pry lunged forward. The slender blade of his sword cane, appearing hardly stronger than a long darning needle, flicked out like the tongue of a snake. The glittering steel embedded itself in the left side of the man's chest.

The man wilted into lifelessness. Blood spurted along the stained steel of the cane as Paul Pry whipped it out and whirled.

The man with the dark, curly hair fired.

The bullet clipped past Paul Pry's body so close that it caught the folds of his coat, tugging and ripping at the garment as though some invisible hand had suddenly snatched at the cloth.

Paul Pry's slender steel flicked out and down. The razor-keen edge cut the tendons on the back of the man's right hand. The nerveless fingers dropped the gun to the floor.

With an oath, he jumped back, flung his left hand under the folds of his coat, whipped out a long-bladed knife.

Paul Pry lunged once more. The man paried the lunge with his knife. Steel grated on steel.

Paul Pry's light blade was turned aside by the heavy knife. The momentum of Pry's lunge carried him forward. The dark-haired man laughed sardonically as he turned the point of the knife toward Paul Pry's throat.

But Paul Pry managed, by a super-human effort, to catch himself just as he seemed on the point of empaling his throat on the knife. His adversary recognized too late that he had lost the advantage. He thrust outward with the knife, but his left hand made the thrust awkward and ill-timed. Paul Pry jumped back from the thrust. Once more the point of his sword cane was flickering in front of him, a glittering menace of steel which moved swiftly.

"So," he said, "you know how to fence?"

The dark-haired man held the heavy knife in readiness to parry the next thrust. "Yes," he said, "I know how to fence far better than you, my friend."

"And I suppose," said Paul Pry, "that is the knife which accounted for the men whose lips were sewed together."

"Just a little trade mark of mine," admitted the man with the knife. "When I leave here, your lips and Thelma's lips will be sewed in the same manner. I'll drop your bodies . . ."

Paul Pry moved with bewildering swiftness. The point of his narrow steel blade darted forward.

The man flung the knife into a position to parry the thrust. "Clumsy," he said.

But Paul Pry's wrist deflected the point at just the proper moment to slide the slender steel just inside the blade of the heavy knife.

The dark-haired man had time to register an expression of bewildered consternation. Then Pry's flicking bodkin buried itself in his heart, and his face ceased to show any expression whatever.

Fifty Grand

Mugs Magoo stared with wide eyes at Paul Pry as he entered the apartment. "Say something," he pleaded.

Paul Pry smiled, took off his hat and coat. "What shall I say?"

"Anything," Mugs Magoo said, "just so I can tell that your lips aren't stuck together with cross-stitches."

Paul Pry took a cigarette case from his pocket, took out a cigarette and inspected the end critically. "Well, Mugs," he said, "suppose I smoke? How would that be?"

"That'd be all right," said Mugs. "Where were you last night?"

"Oh, just around doing things," said Paul Pry. "I had a couple of young women I had to see off on a plane."

"Good-looking?" asked Mugs Magoo.

"Well," said Paul Pry, "they had mighty fine figures, and if they hadn't been so badly frightened they'd have been pretty good lookers."

"And than what did you do with the early part of the morning?"

"I had to cash a check," said Paul Pry.

"I thought you cashed that one yesterday."

"I did, Mugs, but you see, there was a misunderstanding about the check that I left in its place, so Mr. Hammond sent another check for twenty-five thousand to the same party at General Delivery."

"And why didn't the party get that one?" asked Mugs Magoo.

Paul Pry sighed. "That," he said, "is rather a long story."

Eva Bentley pushed open the door of the glass compartment where she had been taking down the radio calls. "There's a lot of hot stuff coming in over the radio," she said, "about this cross-stitch murder."

Paul Pry puffed complacently on his cigarette. "What is it?" he said. "Can you tell me what's happening?"

"Yes," she said. "There's a broadcast out for the apprehension of two women. One of them is Ellen Tracy and the other is Thelma Peters. They were employed as entertainers and floor girls in a downtown speakeasy."

Paul Pry's face showed no expression other

than a mild curiosity. "Indeed?" he said. "And just what have these two young ladies been doing?"

"The police think," she said, "that they can give valuable information about the cross-stitch murderer. In fact, they think the girls might have been implicated in the murders—perhaps unwillingly."

"And what," asked Paul Pry, with that same expression of polite curiosity in his face, "gives the police that impression?"

"Because," said Eva Bentley, "the police raided the speakeasy on a tip this morning about ten o'clock. They found two bodies in the dressing room which had been occupied by Thelma Peters. The men had evidently fought with a knife and pistol, and there may have been another man present in the room. In fact, the police think there was.

"On one of the bodies the police found a surgeon's needle and some thread of exactly the same kind which was used in making the cross-stitches on the lips of the murder victims. The police started an investigation and are pretty well satisfied the man is the cross-stitch murderer. They found evidence which tied him up with a wholesale murder plot. It seems that he'd been collecting money from half a dozen different million-aires, threatening to murder them if they gave the police any information whatever. The two people who were killed were those who had given the police information, but the cross-stitch murderer figured that he'd kill a couple of millionaires anyway, in order to get the newspaper notoriety which would strike terror into the hearts of his proposed victims."

"Rather a neat scheme," said Paul Pry. "And, by the way, have the police any trace of the two young ladies?"

"Not yet; they've just broadcast a general description."

Paul Pry looked at his wrist watch. "Doubtless," he said, "by this time, the young ladies are far, far away, which, prob-ably, is just as well. Possibly they were in-timidated, by the man for whom they worked, into taking certain isolated steps in connection with a murder campaign, but didn't know just how those steps were con-nected up at the time."

"Perhaps," said Eva Bentley, staring at Paul Pry curiously. "The police have a de-scription, however, of a young man who entered the speakeasy just about the time when the autopsy surgeon estimates the two men were killed. Would you like to hear that description?"

Paul Pry yawned and shook his head. "No," he said, "I don't think so. Really, Miss Bentley, I'm not particularly interested in the cross-stitch murders any more."

Mugs Magoo stared at him with stupefied wonder for a moment, then suddenly reaching out, he grasped the neck of the whiskey bottle in his left hand, and, disdaining the use of a glass, tilted the bottle to his lips, letting the contents gurgle down his throat.